ERNESTO QUIÑONEZ

TAÍNA

Ernesto Quiñonez was born in Ecuador and arrived in New York City with his Puerto Rican mother and Ecuadorian father when he was eighteen months old. He was raised in East Harlem, also known as El Barrio. He is an associate professor at Cornell University.

ALSO BY ERNESTO QUIÑONEZ

Bodega Dreams

Chango's Fire

TAÍNA

ERNESTO QUIÑONEZ

VINTAGE BOOKS
A Division of Penguin Random House LLC
NEW YORK

A VINTAGE BOOKS ORIGINAL, SEPTEMBER 2019

LIBRARY OF CONGRESS CATALOGING-IN-PUBLICATION DATA
Names: Quiñonez, Ernesto, author.
Title: Taína / Ernesto Quiñonez.
Description: New York : Vintage Books, a Division of Penguin Random House LLC, 2019. |
"A Vintage Books original"—Title page verso.
Identifiers: LCCN 2019010283 (print) | LCCN 2019011761 (ebook) | ISBN 9781984897497 (ebook) | ISBN 9781984897480 (pbk.)
Classification: LCC PS3567.U3618 (ebook) | LCC PS3567.U3618 T35 2019 (print) | DDC 813/.54—dc23
LC record available at https://lccn.loc.gov/2019010283

Vintage Books Trade Paperback ISBN: 978-1-9848-9748-0
eBook ISBN: 978-1-9848-9749-7

Book design by Debbie Glasserman

www.vintagebooks.com

Printed in the United States of America
10 9 8 7 6 5 4 3 2 1

THE FIRST BOOK OF JULIO

TAÍNA

Miraculous pregnancies are
stories told by old women, whose circle
you won't let me belong to.

—JOSÉ DONOSO, *THE OBSCENE BIRD OF NIGHT*

Verse 1

AND WHEN AT fifteen Taína Flores became pregnant, she said that maybe some *ángel* had entered her project. Taken the elevator. Punched her floor. Stepped off and left its body so it could drift under her bedroom door like mist. The elders at her Kingdom Hall of Jehovah's Witnesses questioned Taína's mother, Sister Flores, and she vowed that Taína had never been with a man. That she had taught her daughter *"Si es macho, puede."* Sister Flores said that she kept so close an eye on her daughter, she was sure that Taína didn't even masturbate. Her reply had made the elders uncomfortable. They squirmed in their chairs. Though a sin, that couldn't have made Taína pregnant. The elders inquired about Taína's cycles: was she early, late, or did they vary? What type of pads did she use? The adhesive kind or the inserted type that are shaped like a man's organ? By this time all the air had gone flat in Taína's life, and it was her mother who answered all the questions.

The trial went on for weeks. Every Sunday after service the two women were called by the elders into a cold room.

Though embarrassed that the entire congregation was laughing behind her back, Sister Flores stood by her daughter's story. The elders proposed to take Taína to Metropolitan Hospital to confirm that she was no longer a virgin. Still, Taína and Sister Flores refused; time and time again, they refused. "*Dios sabe,*" Sister Flores vowed. "I have told the truth." This left the elders with no choice but to kick both women out of "the Truth."

Afterward, the two women became an odd sight in Spanish Harlem because they never spoke much. To each other or anyone. In the street they walked hand in hand, mother clutching daughter, and made only necessary visits to the supermarket and the Check-O-Mate for welfare benefits. There were places that the two had never been to, like a movie theater, a beauty salon, or a bakery. The women were living in a universe of two, and it seemed that not even crowds could ever disturb them. Not catcalls from the corner boys directed at Taína: *"Mira, ¿to' eso tuyo?"* Not gossip from laundromat women, whose bites were directed at Doña Flores: *"Perras cuidan a sus hijas mejor que esa."*

At school, Taína sat alone and got lost among a sea of teenagers. She never cared for clothes, makeup, popularity, or anything. Like her mother, she would smile when smiled at but not talk back, as if her smile were telling you she was not your enemy but didn't care for your friendship. The boys liked her, they all fell in love with her but soon lost interest when she'd stare at walls or anything in front of her, as if the person talking didn't exist. The boys called her conceited. I wondered if she knew she was beautiful. It's not easy to know if you are beautiful. I wondered what else Taína did not know. Did she not know that her voice was a gift? I'd heard that Taína sang beautifully. That she had made the school chorus. That when she took her solo, everyone felt shivers. In her voice was the origin of music. It starts with a cry like that of a newborn. Then the wailing turns, changes, and it seeps inside your skin and drowns out all your pain. In her voice, Ms. Cahill, the science teacher, had said, everyone saw whom they loved and who loved them back. That they could feel their loved ones, smell their scents. That Taína's voice had woven itself into the fabric of their clothes, that for weeks no matter how much soap or how many times they washed them, echoes would remain. Her voice was fixed into every strand of their hair, too; like cigarette smoke, they'd smell her voice for days. That a black girl had wept and said to Taína that day, "You gave it all to the fire, honey. It was like church." That's what I'd heard. And that's what I wanted. I wanted that sound, that voice, so I could hear love. A sound that people wait their whole lives for. I wanted to see who loved me. But all was lost. And if I remember well, Taína had been in one of my classes. It was biology, and she never sang. She said only one word, "pigeon." The word sounded hard, as if her tongue had never known sweets, and her accent was pregnant with Spanish, as if Taína had just arrived to the United States.

Shame.

They said it was this *bochorno* that had turned Taína and her mother to behave like monks, spending their lives locked in a room doing penance. They said it was this shame that the entire neighborhood knew about that caused Taína to stop singing. It was this shame that the two single women were afraid to face and therefore shut the door on everyone and everything. They said Doña Flores had been the worst of mothers. They said Doña Flores should have known better. That even as a child any mother could see that Taína Flores was going to be beautiful and therefore bring trouble. And when Taína's eyes began to sparkle like lakes in Central Park and her breasts went from things boys made fun of to things boys wanted to hold in the dark, this sort of disaster was certain to happen. A pretty young girl like Taína must be kept under lock and key, and Doña Flores was no stranger to men who waited for unaccompanied girls to enter empty elevators.

After what everyone concluded was a tragedy, counselors from our school were sent to call upon apartment 2B at 514 East 100th Street and First Avenue. Doña Flores never answered the door. Detectives made several visits to take the mandatory report. Doña Flores never answered the door. Social workers knocked. Doña Flores never answered. Soon, to cut down on these unwanted visits, Doña Flores pulled Taína out of school. No papers were filed. No homeschooling was used as the pretext. Taína just stopped attending one day.

Doña Flores was now the only one you'd see on the street, and she was either carrying groceries or going to cash in her welfare benefits at the Check-O-Mate. In time, when the gossip was no longer fresh, Spanish Harlem found new things to talk about. Everyone started treating the two the way they wanted to be treated and left them alone.

The only person I ever saw Doña Flores open her door to was this really, really tall old man. He was about seven feet and always wore a black satin cape with a red lining like that of a nurse. He had large hands, and even though he was old, in his late sixties, I think, his hazel eyes flickered like fireflies. People in the neighborhood called him el Vejigante, like the lanky Puerto Rican folk Devil, but nobody knew much about him. El Vejigante had appeared in Spanish Harlem one day out of the blue, as if he had been inside a drawer for many years. He had first been spotted during last year's Puerto Rican Day Parade dressed as a *vejigante,* and soon he was living in El Barrio. And just like Taína and her mother, he'd keep to himself. The only time he walked the streets was at night.

Many times I visited Taína's apartment door. I lived on the tenth floor, in the same project. I'd take the elevator down and punch the second floor. When I'd step out, my heart would race as if I were about to disturb an infant that should be left sleeping. I'd stealthily walk toward 2B, and when I'd get close enough, I'd place my left ear against it. What I heard was complete silence, as if the apartment were empty and ready to be rented out. I kept my ear glued to the door, and when the neighbor in 2A caught me, she said she had done the same and that I wouldn't hear a thing. That no sounds escaped from underneath the door of 2B, as if not even dead people lived there, for even the dead, she said, made noises.

But I kept visiting her door because I was certain Taína

would become like characters in Bible stories. I had this vision of people from all over the world making pilgrimages to Spanish Harlem so they might, just might, get a glimpse of a pregnant virgin living in the East River projects. They'd place their ears to the door of 2B as I had, and if they were lucky, they might be blessed by hearing a sigh escaping from Taína's saintly lungs. I was so sure this was going to happen. In El Barrio, Taína's story had spread. Many had shrugged, many had laughed, no one believed, but I felt that it was only a matter of time before 2B in 514 on 100th Street would be known as the building that harbored a living saint.

But this didn't happen.

The residents of Spanish Harlem continued to believe in the unfortunate shame, the tragedy, that had befallen Taína. The man who had done this was probably the same man whose pictures once splattered the walls of the Hell Gate Post Office on 110th Street and Lexington Avenue. This man had been going around the neighborhood bargain shopping for young girls like one shops for shoes. This man was known to follow unaccompanied girls all the way to their apartment doors. Come up behind them with a knife, demanding, "Your life or your eyes?" This man had brought harm all over the neighborhood, and many believed he was the father of Taína's child.

But I didn't.

I believed Taína.

I believed in Taína. And when the man who many said was the father was caught and sent away, I took all the money my mother had given me to buy new jeans and sneakers and caught the Metro-North up to Ossining, New York. I had his name from reading *El Diario*. I had never visited a prison before, so I naïvely thought that since I knew his name, I could just show up like it was a hospital and say I was here to visit Orlando Castillo and be let inside. The guard told me that I needed an adult who was family to this Orlando Castillo. And that I could come only when the inmate was scheduled to receive visits. I said to the guard that I just wanted to ask the man one question, that it would not take long, but the guard had no time for me. There were tons of families waiting in line to sign in so they could hop on a bus that drove them to the compound. I was holding up the line. The guard told me that I better leave or he would kick my punk ass out.

I left angry because it had been a long and expensive trip, a train and then a bus, but most important I had no answer to my question: "Did you ever visit 2B in 514 and First Avenue? A project in Spanish Harlem by the East River? She is about fifteen, with hazel eyes?" I was sure that that man would've said "no," or most likely he'd lie and say that he couldn't remember.

I began to question why had I taken so much interest in Taína. Why I couldn't sleep, eat, or believe in anything that contradicted my true hope that Taína had conceived a child all by herself. Was it believing that she was a virgin, in some way, my idea of keeping her all to myself? Of course I was in love with her. But even at seventeen, I felt something inside me, in a place that I hardly knew was there, tell me that this interest in Taína was more than just a crush, it was more like a sadness one feels for neglected children or books or flowers. A sadness like a *coquí* that has been told to remain silent and I wanted Taína to sing.

AT SCHOOL EVERYONE would laugh at me, especially Mario De Puma. He'd slap the back of my neck at lunchtime.

"Seventeen? And you don't know how babies are made, psycho?"

Of course I knew, but Mario was big and I could never win in a fight.

"It was a miracle," I'd say.

Mario would then take the ice cream from my tray and laugh some more. "The only virgin here is you." All the other boys looked away, relieved that it wasn't them Mario was picking on.

Though I was a virgin, I'd respond that sex had nothing to do with it. "Were you there, psycho?" he'd say with a mouth full of ice cream. "Fuck no, right? So how'd you know?"

"Other people were there."

"Fuck you." He spat some out on the ground to clear his throat. "Everyone knows you hear things, you hear voices in your big head."

"I do not hear voices." Because I did not. I did see things, but they were my way of dealing with my life. The things I saw, my visions, my daydreams, were there for me and only me. "Mario, what about people surviving airplanes falling from the sky? You know? Things that can't be explained."

"You sound like such a psycho fag." And he'd throw

what he hadn't eaten at my face. "I've known you since the fourth grade. You thought syphilis was an X-Men." Mario laughed and walked away.

But I did not care. The ridicule was nothing. I soon began to worry about Taína's unborn child. I started to save all my allowance, five dollars a week. I began buying gifts for her unborn child. I bought baby shoes, baby clothes, Pampers, baby lotion, talcum powder, baby oil, wipes, baby shampoo. I would leave them at Taína's door. The next day I'd always find my gifts lying on the cold cement next to the uncollected trash bags.

One day while walking down the street, I saw a secondhand crib in the window of an Army-Navy pawnshop. It was made of beautiful oak with angels carved on the headboard. The crib was a bit expensive and I could never save enough to buy it, so I bought a bassinet that lay next to it. I carried it home, hiding it from my parents, all the while wondering if Taína's stomach was as round as the moon. As with all my previous gifts, I leaned the bassinet quietly in front of Taína's door. I then rang the doorbell and hid in the stairwell like a Halloween prankster. The door opened and my heart jumped. But it was not Taína or her mother, but el Vejigante. This tall old man looked both ways, as if he knew someone was hiding. He then grunted as if smoke and fire could arise from his nostrils. El Vejigante picked up the bassinet, turned it around, rubbed it, and then placed it right back where I had left it and slammed the door shut.

The next day I found the bassinet in the street with the rest of the uncollected trash and junked furniture.

I kept trying, but neither Doña Flores nor Taína would

open. I'd knock and place my ear to the door. I'd knock, sometimes politely whisper, "Taína?" or, "Taína, it's Julio, we were in biology, you there?" And not even an eye would stare back from the peephole. I'd then ride the elevator back up to the tenth floor, feeling as empty as the space between the stars.

Verse 2

WHO OR WHAT is the Thing that orders an atom to join another so as to form a sperm cell and not wood, metal, or air? Who is responsible for the development of a child as it floats in all that goo of darkness? Even at seventeen, I felt God was not the answer. He was too large. Anything could be placed inside Him without really fitting in. What I was after was for someone to explain this miracle to me, to draw me a chart so I could see it down to its most minor of minor details. For it was only there, in the smallest of places, among all that unfilled space that exists between one atom and another, it must be there, where Taína could conceive a child all by herself. What if something revolutionary had happened? What if somewhere in the infinity of inner space, some atom got fed up? What if this atom declared it would no longer follow the laws written in Taína's DNA? What if this atom started a revolution in Taína's body? What if other atoms decided they would join that revolution, and instead of creating the cell they were supposed to—created a sperm cell? And as the revolution became more popular, trillions and trillions of trillions of atoms followed suit until the rebellion invaded Taína's womb by means of self-created sperm?

"*¡Ay bendito!* Are you hearing voices?" My mother, hands shot up in the air, mouth wide-open, couldn't accept my explanation. "*Pa'* Lincoln Hospital is where I'm taking you. *Pa'* Lincoln," she said, looking up at the ceiling as if God could hear. But God couldn't, so she looked over at my Ecuadorian father, who could.

"*¿Ves? ¿Ves?* Silvio," she said as we sat at the dinner table, "that's because of you talking of revolutions since he was little."

"He is a man," my father said in Spanish, because my father talked only in Spanish. He was already done eating and was now reading the Ecuadorian newspaper *El Universo*. My father was unemployed. He read all newspapers not just for want ads but for distraction, even read the papers from my mother's country of Puerto Rico. "He is a man. Leave my son alone."

I remember feeling proud that my father had called me a man. I wanted to be a man. Taking care of Taína or at least believing in her made me feel like I was acting out my role. Who or what had given me this role? I didn't know. But just like those Buddhist monks who couldn't explain what nirvana was, they just knew when they had reached it, I knew this was what I was supposed to do.

My mother sighed loudly. She turned on the kitchen radio, low volume. She used to be a *salsera* but now loved songs from bygone times. Tito Rodríguez sang, *Tiemblas, cada vez que me ves.*

And then she faced me again.

"Julio, Taína was . . . touched." My mother could never say certain words, as if saying them would make their definitions enter our home.

"I don't believe that, Ma."

"He is now eighteen, he is a man," my father repeated without missing a black letter on the printed page. "Either take him to the hospital or let him make up his own world."

"See, Ma." I nodded and pointed in Pops's direction. "He gets it."

"Tu pa no sabe na' "—she paused—"because you're not eighteen."

"So, almost, seventeen and a half—"

"Oh, big man," Mom said, inflating her chest.

"Leonor." My father placed the newspaper down for a second. "You took him to church. You told him that one man, just one man, ruined the perfect plan of God. So, believe Julio and his revolutionary atom."

"Oh, *entonces*"—she crossed her arms—"you believe in Julio's revolutionary atom?"

"No. But I do not believe that you came out of my rib either."

"That's different," Mom snapped, "Adam and Eve were real! *La Biblia es verdad.* What Julio is talking about is crazy talk. That's how crazy people talk."

"He is in love," Pops said, and it embarrassed me. "That is all. My son is in love."

"No, I'm not," I lied. "I don't like Taína. I like older girls," I said, as if I had to convince myself.

"*No, señorito,* love or no love you better leave those

women alone. I knew Taína's mother, *esa Inelda está loca. ¿Me oyes?*"

"Yeah, yeah, Ma, I heard, I heard, she used to be a great singer and went crazy, you told me. You two were friends before she went crazy, I heard. And I'm not in love, okay?"

"So, you're not in love, eh?" My mother pointed at my food.

My father looked at my full plate.

"You take after your mother," Pops said. "Out of all Latinos, it is Puerto Ricans." Pops picked up the newspaper that lay aside on the table. He flipped through *El Vocero* and laughed. "Look at this, you Puerto Ricans believe in Chupacabras, aliens in El Yunke, *espiritismo*—"

"*Oh sí, pero ¿quién lee eso?* So you must like it," Mom said, ripping the paper from his hands and rolling it into a cylinder. She then hit Pops over the head with it.

Pops laughed, looking at the rolled-up newspaper.

"Leonor," he said, "you would have made a great union buster, the way you handle that newspaper." Mom made believe she was about to whack him again, but she smiled lovingly.

"Now, in my country," my father said, looking my way, "you had to choose sides and stick with that choice." My father was really talking about his youthful communist days in Ecuador, but I could place what he said only in context to what I was going through in my own life. I had chosen to believe that Taína was telling the truth. I would not go back no matter what common sense was handed to me. There were things that took time to be understood. All I had to do was hold the fort until something or someone would come and help me in helping others understand what had happened to Taína.

"Okay, *basta,*" Mom said to my father. *"Tú me vas a dar un patatú."* Mom then looked my way again. "And you"—she pointed a forefinger like God as she opened a kitchen cabinet and took out the Windex—"you better not get me in trouble with my elders again. You better stop going down to the second floor and spying on those women and that crazy old man."

"I don't know that old man," I said, "I don't know anything about el Vejigante. I just think Taína is telling the truth."

"Well, she's not, and I don't like that Taína." She squeezed twice, and Windex spat on our glass kitchen table. "And that old man, no one knows anything about him because he must like it that way and that means he is hiding secrets," Mom said, waxing the glass clean.

Y por eso tiemblas . . . Tito Rodríguez sang.

When my mother said the word "secrets," my father's eyes left the newspaper and shot them at her. He was telling Mom something and she didn't want to hear it, so she didn't look back at him. I knew their games of dealing with each other, and at times it made me mad so I just let it be.

"Those people are hiding secrets, Julio."

"You don't hide secrets, Ma," I said. "That's like a double negative or something?"

My father cleared his throat and seriously continued to look at my mother. "We know about things," he said, "things we hide." Whatever he was referring to, Mom did not like it. She wanted to say something back but jailed her tongue. He stared at her intensely a bit longer, and when she didn't say anything, that was enough. He won. Whatever it was, Mom did not want to go there, wherever it was that Pops was headed. So she continued to polish the kitchen, singing along to Tito Rodríguez's smoky "Puerto Rican Sinatra" voice. Together they sang the story of a woman who trembles when she sees the singer, and why does she continue to hide that she is part of him?

Verse 3

IT HAD BECOME a habit. I'd wait for my parents to go to bed and then sneak out of our apartment. Out by the lonely hallway I'd punch for the elevator. Wait. Get in. Step out and open the project's entrance doors and go out onto the sidewalk. I'd then cross the street and face our building, but instead of looking up ten flights to find my bedroom, I'd simply gaze up at Taína's lonely second-floor window. I would lean on a blue mailbox and see Taína's shades drawn, the lights always low. I'd stand there long enough to see many of our project's windows go black.

One fall night as I leaned on the mailbox, staring up at Taína's window from across the street, I saw two silhouettes step out of our project. It was late and dark, but I could see a fat figure holding on to the skinnier one with this grace and I knew it was Taína and her mother.

My heart jumped like a dolphin.

I hadn't seen Taína and here she was. It took all my strength to not cross the street and scare them away. I wanted to be near Taína, but I feared that if her mother saw me, they'd go right back up. What were they doing out so late? Where were they going? Maybe Taína needed her exercise, I thought. Maybe she needed to stay healthy so she could have a good birth. This was how she must get fresh air, I thought. Taína must come out at night so no one bothers her. No one sees her. The two women had shut themselves off from the rest of the world, and like owls they felt comfortable flying when everyone else was asleep.

From across the street I saw Taína's semi-brown semi-blond hair was frizzed like she had just gotten out of bed. Her hair hinted at being charged with electricity and there was a static glow rising from her frizz like a halo. Her coat was woolly and oversize, as if out of impatience she simply took the first one at hand. Her coat was a cloak, like she wasn't so much cold but needed something large to hide inside of. I followed behind all the way from 100th Street and First Avenue to 106th Street and Third. Once we left the enclave of the projects, the night came alive. The new residents of Spanish Harlem had come out to take in all that new nightlife. There were lots of bars and cafés opened till late where all these young, mostly white people ate, drank, and laughed in what they were now calling Spa-Ha. But even among the new residents I didn't lose sight of the two women. From across the street I saw them turn the corner. He had been waiting for them, standing tall as ever, wearing his black cape and carrying a walking stick. El Vejigante kissed both women on the cheek twice like Europeans and hugged them like he was their father. They spoke for a few seconds before continuing to walk, casting this strange wide shadow like misshapen squares. They didn't walk but rather strolled like they were taking in sun in Central Park and not out past midnight. At times I could hear Doña Flores laugh a little at what el Vejigante was saying. Soon, all three went inside a twenty-four-hour bodega. I crossed the street, and from outside the bodega's window, I saw Taína pick up a glossy magazine and her mother some nail polish remover. El Vejigante didn't look at anything and just waited by the cash register. I shifted my weight and squinted my eyes to see what the title of the magazine was that Taína had picked up, but I couldn't read the cover. I soon realized that it wasn't nail polish remover but *agua maravilla* that Doña Flores had gotten. At the counter, Doña Flores placed Taína's magazine, the witch hazel, and a pack of Twinkies Taína had wanted. El Vejigante flipped his cape aside and dug into his pocket. He didn't seem to have a lot of money because he paid in coins, like he had broken his piggy bank. After that, I hid behind a parked car as all three left the store, and el Vejigante must have asked Taína something because she nodded and smiled.

Walking, Taína no longer held her mother's arm. She unwrapped her Twinkies. Taína ate them in big bites like they were hot dogs, and after licking her fingers clean, she began to walk slower as she flipped through the pages of her magazine in a way that let me know she was only looking at the pictures. Maybe because it was nighttime she couldn't read, but after three more blocks, she was done and she gave the magazine to el Vejigante, who took it and rolled it up nicely as if he didn't want to ruin it. Taína held on to her mother once again and the two continued to walk side by side.

Third Avenue was lit by its lampposts and the late fall night was cool. When they reached the playground on 107th Street, Taína and her mother walked inside, but el Vejigante did not. He waited outside the gates of the playground as if he could not enter because he had been forbidden to cross some invisible line. He simply stood outside the playground's fence, not even sitting on the benches, standing as if he had been a dog left tied to a parking meter. Taína then chose a swing, and even though her stomach was big she sat on the swing with no problem. Doña Flores began to push her from behind so Taína could gather more speed and her swing could climb higher. It was then that I heard Taína playfully yell at her mother the word *"sí."* And I was so happy to have heard Taína speak, and I became afraid that some act of God or something might interrupt this moment by taking me away. I started to sweat, but then, all of a sudden, this anxiety left me and some mysterious change came over me as if I knew everything was going to be all right.

Doña Flores kept pushing Taína's swing. Taína's legs were dangling and she'd bend them down and then straighten them up to gather speed while holding on tight to the swing's chains. Taína threw her head back, letting the wind take hold of her hair, and then I heard Taína speak again, "No." Two words. I knew Taína could sing beautifully and maybe she would right there and then. A cappella was just as good. I was so excited knowing I would see who loved me or maybe even have one of my visions. But her swing soon came to a halt. Her mother asked her something and Taína nodded, and the two women left the playground to rejoin el Vejigante outside the fence.

I was a half block behind when they turned toward the East River and back toward home. El Vejigante continued to walk like he was on a stroll, though the two women were now walking with their heads down, making sure no one saw them. Even this late, even with the streets this empty of native residents and mostly filled with young white people, they began to walk without making eye contact with cars, lampposts, mailboxes, buildings, or anything.

In no time, all three reached our project building on 100th Street and First Avenue, and all three went inside and I was alone again.

I was happy at having been so close to Taína, and it had taken all my strength not to yell, "Hi." I looked around at the wall of projects surrounding me. I smiled because among all those square windows that lent the projects its definitions, inside one of those cubes lived a saint. And then somewhere underneath uncollected garbage bags, I heard a cricket calling out for love. I looked down at the concrete and felt like all the garbage bags, the candy wrappers, coffee cups, oil slicks, broken glass, gum stains, cigarette ends, pizza boxes, all the cans, all this garbage, were telling me that these things loved me. I belonged to them. That even though I was from the projects, this world could still love me, embrace me, and make me feel valuable and not like an unwanted child.

And then it brought me comfort to know that all these buildings full of poor people lived close to a river. A real river, the East River, and for some reason I started to walk toward the water. When I reached the East River, I realized for the first time how only the FDR Drive divided the projects from the water's boardwalk. The cars on the highway sped by me, sounding like waves.

"Don't be afraid, *papo*." El Vejigante startled me. He held a crowbar in one hand. I slowly backed away. I was ready to run when he caught my eyes looking at the iron. I sensed he felt embarrassed.

"Take it." El Vejigante held the crowbar out toward me. "Take it, *papo*."

I snatched it from his hand, though I knew I could never hit him. I held the crowbar like a baseball bat that I was willing to swing at any moment.

"Now I hope you're not scared now, *papo*?" he said with his hands in front, in case I did swing. He was old but tall; it gave him the appearance of having a lot of life left in him. He was light-skinned, and it was in the way he called me *papo* that I knew he was one hundred percent Puerto Rican, like my mom.

"Many people don't know me because old people are invisible." He laughed a little laugh. He had a huge gap between his front teeth. Being close to him, I saw that his cape was worn out, the satin fading. His pants were thin, as was his shirt, the fabrics disappearing into strings. His hair was long, split in the middle, and held together with a rubber band. That night when I first talked to him, he reminded me of a broken-down Jesus Christ, ragged, old, and fallen, whose disciples had long ago deserted him.

"What you want?" I said, though what I wanted was to ask him about Taína.

"Me?" He slouched the way tall people do when they

feel inferior for being so tall. "Me? I'd like to begin again. But you see, you can't do that, *papo*."

"Okay," I said, because I didn't know what he was talking about. I gripped the crowbar tighter just to give me something to do.

"You're Julio, right? You live in Taína's project, like eight floors up?" he asked, and I nodded. "I've seen you around." His voice was all gravel like those fancy coffee machines.

"So what?" I said.

"No, it's good. You believe Taína is telling the truth—"

"She is telling the truth," I interrupted. "You know her, so you know she is telling the truth."

"Okay, okay, okay, calm down," he said, because I didn't know I had raised my voice.

"I'm sorry"—my voice lowered—"are you Taína's father?" Though he was too old to be, I asked.

"No, no, no. No." He crouched, hunching his shoulders like he was humbling himself. "You want those women to talk to you, *papo*?" And though his hazel eyes still sparkled, his face was riddled with wrinkles.

I shrugged like I didn't care.

"Don't be like that." He knew I was playing it off. Trying to be cool about it.

"I don't trust you," I said. It was late, and I needed to get home before my parents woke up.

"I don't blame you. Trust is hard, *papo*, but okay," he said. "Meet me tomorrow night, *papo*. Same time, across from Taína's window by the mailbox, and I'll tell you what to do. I'll tell you what to do so they can open the door, okay?"

I nodded.

And he turned around, about to walk away.

"Hey, you want your crowbar back?" I said, and he turned to face me again.

"Yeah, I might be able to sell it."

"Vejigante"—I gave him back the iron—"what's your real name?"

"Me?" He took his crowbar and looked up at the night sky, as if he could find his name in the stars. He then looked down at the concrete, then at the highway of cars passing by, then at the night sky again, as if he weren't sure where to start or what to say. When he did face me, his hazel eyes were huge, like an Egyptian's eye in those mummy coffins at the Met. He scanned my face like a nervous radar, debating if he should tell me.

"M-m-my, real name is Sal-Salvador," he stuttered a bit. "My mother when she was alive"—and he crossed himself—"would call me Sal. But once when I was about your age, I was famous."

"Really?"

"Yeah. I was all over the papers, *papo*. *Time* magazine, *Newsweek*. When I was your age," he said in the saddest of sad tones, "I was the Capeman."

THE SECOND BOOK OF JULIO

THE CAPEMAN

In a couple of days they come and take me away.

—PAUL SIMON, "ME AND JULIO DOWN BY THE SCHOOLYARD"

Verse 1

MY FRIENDS AND I were sitting at our corner of the lunchroom. They served pizza and ice cream. I was holding court.

"Can't you guys see, like something happened inside, really, really, inside her body and it produced sperm cells instead of blood cells or skin cells or bone cells, or anything like that."

"No way," BD said.

"Why not? It supposedly already happened once, right?" I said.

"Yeah, but that was God." BD had lost an arm because of his need for trouble. His mother would actually want him to sleep in, to wake up late in the afternoon, because then he'd have less time to get into trouble.

"God had nothing to do with it," I said.

BD had lost his arm on a dare. Some kid challenged him to jump down the subway tracks of the 103rd Street stop and walk across from one platform to the other. BD survived when the train came out of nowhere, but he did lose an arm. Because of his prosthetic limb, everyone in

Spanish Harlem stopped calling him Hector and called him Bionic Dude. In his pocket, BD always carried a picture of himself when he had both arms to show everyone that he wasn't born that way.

"Things can happen only once," Sylvester said. "I lost my virginity. See, only once."

And we snapped, "You wish!"

Sylvester's real name was Elvis, but when he talked, he gave you the weather. The guy spat all over the place. No one called him Elvis. Instead everyone called him Sylvester like the spitting cat in cartoons. He was not really my friend *because* he was the worst person to eat with, but he was not a bad guy. And he never returned the pencils he'd borrowed, and if he did, they had teeth marks on them.

"Listen, all I'm saying is our moms drag us to church every Sunday to hear about something like this happening. And it's happening again, today."

"You crazy," BD said.

"Everyone knows she was attacked," Sylvester spat. We covered our trays.

"She was not," I said, and wiped my arm where some spit had landed. "Her mother said she was not. Her mother keeps an eye on her like twenty-four/seven. So she should know. And I know for sure because I went to see that dude who attacked those girls."

"That's bullshit." BD was about to dig in his pocket for Jolly Ranchers.

"That's right, and I talked with him in prison and he said he didn't do it."

"Yeah, but that's what all convicts say, man," he said

with a mouthful of meat loaf. "Everyone says they didn't do it." Sylvester spat chunks.

"Didn't I just say I talked with that guy—"

"How you get there?" BD asked.

"My father drove me, and I went inside that prison. It was just like on TV, a lot of skinheads, Aryan Nations, Bloods, tattoo guys lifting weights and stuff. Just like in *Cops*." I was happy when they believed me.

"Hey, okay, fine," Sylvester said, "but he ain't the only rapo around. Maybe it was some other guy who did it."

"No way," I said.

"Yo, listen," BD said, "her *toto* was invaded, that's it, all right."

"I don't know why you Dominicans call it *toto,*" Sylvester spat at BD. "Shouldn't it be *tota*?"

"Fuck you, why don't you go give the weather somewhere else?" BD said.

"No, why do you Dominicans call it *toto*?" Sylvester drank some milk. "That's like male. See, in PR we called it *chocha,* see, that's female." And milk rained.

"Can you guys shut the fuck up," I said.

With his good arm BD brought out Jolly Ranchers from his pocket. "Want some?"

We took one.

"You know Taína can sing, right? Right?" I said.

"I was there," BD said. "I heard her."

"You were there?" I was excited to hear this. "You never told me, BD."

"Me and Sylvester were both there. Man, there was no more room at typing. So they had to accept us at chorus.

Whack." BD laughed. "When the class saw Sylvester walk in they all moved to the opposite side of the room."

"That's bullshit!" Sylvester rained spit defending himself. "I can carry a note, motherfuckah."

"Yeah, but you a fire hydrant, bro," BD said. "And everyone knew it. But Taína was the only one who didn't move. She just sat there and waited for her part."

"What happened?" My best friend had actually been there. I wanted to hear all about it. "What happened? What happened?"

"Nothing." BD shrugged. "She sang. It was good. That's all. That's the last I ever heard her talk or anything."

"That's it?" I said. "But Ms. Cahill said all these things about her singing."

"Nah," BD said, "it was just singing."

"See, that's why you don't know shit 'bout music, BD," Sylvester said. "Yeah, all right, I might spit a little bit, but—"

"A little bit? Nigga, you got tsunamis coming out of your mouth."

"Let 'im talk, BD," I said, because Sylvester had been there, too. "Let 'im talk."

"Thank you, Julio," Sylvester said. "Cuz BD don't know shit about music, but I know music. I know cuz when that girl got up to sing it was like a radio had been turned on. Ms. Cahill and everyone outside in the hallway came into the music room to hear. They had a face like 'Holy shit, this ugly duckling is a swan.' "

"Taína is not ugly," I said, "but what else?"

"She hit like six or seven octaves." Sylvester then looked at BD. "You know what an octave is?"

"Yeah, it's when your mother fucks an octopus."

"What else, Sylvester, what else?" I said.

"It was beautiful, man. Then she clammed up, never heard another word from her."

"Didn't sing again?"

"Didn't speak again," Sylvester said.

Just then we all tensed up. Mario was coming our way.

Mario De Puma, the Italian kid we had grown up with. He was now twenty years old, a super-duper super-senior. He had a year left before he'd turn twenty-one and the public school system could legally kick him out. Mario was like the Incredible Hulk from the comic books that he was always reading. He was stocky, but all muscles. His hands looked like they could tear the phone book in two. He lived by Pleasant Avenue, next to Rao's restaurant, the last stronghold of the old Little Italy section in Spanish Harlem. Everyone knew his father because he was just like Mario, not very bright but a boulder of a man. Some said Mario's father had been an enforcer for John Gotti.

During lunchtime Mario would play out this scene. He'd pace around the table where my friends and I were still eating. His hand held an opened pint of milk. We knew he was going to pour milk on one of us.

That day when we spotted Mario coming, we all stopped talking, held on to the Jolly Ranchers in our mouths, and stared ahead, hoping to not be the one Mario chose to pick on. But I felt his presence behind me. He hated me, called me psycho. Then I felt the cold milk being poured down my neck, running down my back and into my jeans.

I heard Mario laugh.

"Don't get mad. You're a wetback anyway," he said. "Don't get up. Mexican, Puerto Rican, Dominican, all wetbacks."

But I shot up and seriously looked straight at him.

"Oh, shit, it's you, psycho." He didn't know. "What you gonna do? I'll hit you so hard your children will be born dizzy."

I wanted to hit Mario, though I knew he'd kill me.

I slowly sat back down.

"I'll tell you something about that Taína, psycho," he said really loud so the whole lunchroom could hear, "I did that dumb box. I'm the father." And then Mario laughed, walking away really proud of himself as if he had just slaughtered some big game.

"I got a sweater in my backpack you can borrow," BD said, "or you can use it as a towel."

But I was furious and felt like crying. The milk was running down my back, becoming colder as it wet my underwear.

I WANTED TO be part of Taína's life. I wanted to be able to somehow make Taína's breaths coincide with my heartbeats, the way I had read some Buddhist monks did with the universe. So that even when the monks were sleeping, their heartbeats were in tune with all things. I wanted to feel like that. To always have Taína beating inside me. To one day hear her sing and see love, really see love, coming through her lungs. But Taína had shut herself off from the world, and el Vejigante knew.

I needed to know more about him. So, after school I visited the Aguilar public library on 110th Street and Lexington. I knew what a *vejigante* was and why they called him that. The old man was tall and skinny, like he walked on stilts. But I didn't know who the Capeman was. I sat at a computer and googled that name.

The pictures that came on-screen were of a skinny kid not much different from me only way taller, with hazel eyes, and in handcuffs. His full name was Salvador Negron, born in Mayagüez, Puerto Rico. He was shuffled from New York City and back to the island by his parents as many times as he would later be shuffled from juvenile detention center to juvenile detention center. From prisons to asylums to prisons once again.

Wikipedia said that it was the last year of the fifties. The New York City streets belonged to doo-wop groups and teenage gangs. Some, like the Vampires, were both. They choose a subway platform, throw a hat on the cement, snap their fingers, and soon a cappella grooves would be bouncing off the subway walls. They added melody and harmony to the underground, and many gangs made a few dollars this way. It was common knowledge, a known rule among the doo-wop gangs, that the subway was for all, but above ground, the singing street corners were turf wars. As the lead singer of the Vampires, Salvador liked to choose singing corners that other doo-wop gangs considered theirs.

It was late in evening when the playground killings occurred. All over the Upper West Side from the 100s down to the 70s, the large population of Puerto Ricans that lived there before gentrification, before the cleaning of Needle

Park, was taking in the street nightlife of radios blasting salsa. Of opened fire hydrants. Everyone looking for someone to dance with, looking for someone to love and to be loved in return. Everyone cooling off from a summer heat wave. It was later in the evening when word arrived to Salvador that some kids from a doo-wop white gang, the Norsemen, had beaten up a Puerto Rican member. As lead singer and president of the Vampires, Salvador rounded up his boys. He instructed the Vampires to meet on the Norsemen's turf, a playground on 46th Street and Ninth Avenue where the Vampires would sometimes sing without any permission.

Some Vampires came walking, some took the bus. Salvador jumped the turnstiles and took the 1 train, got off at 42nd Street, and then headed west. He was wearing his cape and he carried a dagger along with all that hate, anger, betrayal, and abuse—a wealth of tragedies just waiting for an excuse to be set free. It was a moonless midnight in a New York City neighborhood known back then as Hell's Kitchen. The playground was dark. The lampposts were broken. Doing nothing but hanging out by the swings were a couple of white boys.

"Hey, no Norsemen in this playground," Salvador yelled at them, feeling all right. He was with his boys, with his troops. Like when he sang lead, his Vampires were backing him up. The white boys ran. Salvador and his Vampires chased and fell on two of them. Salvador kicked one of them down and started screaming at his face, "This is our playground. No Norsemen! No white Norsemen!" His dagger stabbed the white boy. And then Salvador stabbed the other boy, too . . . but these boys were not the Norsemen. They were not gang members. They were just innocent white teenage boys hanging out at this playground at night.

Bleeding a crimson river, the first teen made it to the entrance of a tenement building. He knocked on a first-floor apartment, and an old Irish lady quickly recognized him as one of the boys from the neighborhood. The old lady knelt down. Held the bloodied body in her arms as if she wanted to give him what was left of her life. He in turn closed his eyes, made garbled noises like a baby learning to talk, and died in her old arms.

The second bleeding teen made it to his apartment building across the playground. He managed to drag himself up a flight of stairs and knock at his apartment door. His mother opened it and found her bloodied son gasping for breath like a coughing radiator. She held him, crying, as he died in the hallway.

This was what Wikipedia said, and many of the pictures on the computer screen showed a handcuffed, tall, skinny kid at the police precinct wearing a cape just like the one el Vejigante wore. His eyes were angry and red, as if he had been crying a dry, angry cry that burns your throat.

This happened a long time ago in my city, though I could not recognize it, yet it was the same city, and the kid on the screen looked nothing like el Vejigante did today. He was just a kid whom the media called the Capeman.

I logged off.

I was not scared by what el Vejigante had done when he was my age. I was still determined to meet him later that night because I would do anything to be part of Taína's life.

Hear her sing. But one thing had scared me. It was what Salvador was quoted as saying that night, long ago, when public rage demanded blood, the Capeman's blood, and called for execution by electric chair.

"I don't care if I burn," the Capeman said. "My mother can watch."

Verse 2

THE THINGS THE Capeman had said about his mother had stayed with me. Mom had warned me not to visit Taína. I wondered what she would do if she knew about el Vejigante's past. And me talking to him. And meeting him later that night. Mom would always say, "*Pa'* Lincoln Hospital is where I'm taking you. *Pa'* Lincoln, *otra vez, pa'* Lincoln." And I'd get a bit scared because I had been to that hospital a few times and never liked it. Mom had taken me to the psych ward when I was thirteen after I said that Jesus was stupid for curing the blind. What he should have done was cure blindness. Jesus was also dumb for bringing Lazarus back from the dead. Why not just get rid of death? Made sense to me. But Mom said that what Jesus did was show a taste of what the Kingdom of God will bring. I said, Why wait? Just bring it. Mom got mad, and so off to Lincoln Hospital we went. She missed a day's work, too, and told the doctor that I heard voices and acted as if I were crazy.

Yes, I do see things. I do. I do have visions; some people call them daydreams, but mine are vivid and they help me.

The things I see are there to help me and no one else. I don't force them on anybody. I told this to the doctor, and he nodded and then scheduled more appointments.

I remember a skinny girl during one of my visits. She had tried to kill herself by drinking Drano. She was interned at the ward. Received some money from somewhere, but no one visited her. She couldn't go outside or down to the cafeteria to buy candy bars. She'd always ask visitors if they could go to the cafeteria on the ground floor and get her Snickers. She even had the money in hand. All she needed was for someone to go and get the chocolates because the doctors wouldn't let her out. During one of my doctor visits, I brought Snickers bars with me and a nurse saw them. She said not to give them to the skinny girl. I listened to the nurse. Twice a month Mom would take me for my sessions with the shrink and I'd see the skinny girl. At first I thought that they were doing the skinny girl a favor because of weight issues, but that wasn't it. "She will say they are stale. Throw them at your face," the nurse told me, "and then yell curses and it will be us who will have to put up with her. Not you. Us. So don't buy her any chocolates, please." But I'd still bring Snickers, and one day I decided to give them to the skinny girl. She thanked me. She even paid me and went to a corner of the visiting lounge to look out the window. She savored every bite, happy to be eating by the large window of the visitors' lounge that is the pride of Lincoln Hospital's psychiatric ward. The lounge's window showcases all the projects of the South Bronx blending in with the wealthy New York City skyline looming at a distance. The skinny girl sat there as if she were watching a movie about two different cities living in one. Sometimes she would happily laugh to herself. The nurses and doctors were wrong. That's when I wanted never to return to Lincoln Hospital. I began to lie to the doctor. I told him what he wanted to hear. That I did not see any more visions. That his sessions were working. His pills, too, though I faked taking them. Soon, the doctor said I should return only if I heard voices or started to see things again. Great. No more visits, and just to be safe I told my mother that Christ was good, a pretty awesome dude. I mean, when the wine ran out, he turned water into wine so the party could go on, who could not love this guy? Hung out with whores and never beat, robbed, or jammed them. Great guy. He should be cloned. Yes, a true superstar. I even went with her to Kingdom Hall meetings, and that's where I first noticed Taína.

I TRULY BELIEVED that a revolution had taken place in Taína's body. No one had touched her. She was telling the truth. The fact that no one believed Taína made her pure and her story true.

One day while taking the number 6 train to school, I had a vision.

I saw Taína.

She was in her house.

It was early morning.

Taína woke up. Her body was feeling strange. She did not know what it was, but it was something. So she took an aspirin and made herself a peanut-butter-and-jelly sandwich and drank water. But soon Taína felt hyperaware—the beating of her heart, the fringe of her eyelashes, the expansion and deflation of her lungs—her body was talking to her. In my vision I saw Taína blink and stop chewing because the world suddenly appeared shimmery, blurred, and melting. All things around her seemed out of focus, as if something inside her had unexpectedly shifted. Taína took a deep breath full of fear and panic. Her heart pounded like it wanted to break her rib cage. Then, all of a sudden she felt light, this unbearable lightness of being, as if she needed more water because the weight of the liquid would keep her from levitating. Then, a deep clarity inside her inner universe whispered to her that it was okay to relax, it whispered that she was only pregnant. That a revolution had ignited inside her. An atom had decided to revolt in order to create life. This atom did not want to dwell in the infinity of Taína's inner space and do as told. This atom did not want to shift its orbit or give up electrons when bonding with another atom in order to create the molecule it was supposed to. This atom felt the need, the desire, to use its electricity and its endless resource of nearby atoms to convince them that they are the building blocks of the cosmos and so they have the power to start again in a whole new body. Together, trillions of trillions of trillions of rebellious atoms drew up a blueprint. They would no longer do as it was written in the laws of Taína's DNA or any law. They would now be the ones to decide what compound bonds to form, how many electrons and neutrons to include or exclude or share in their compositions, all with the ending goal of creating life. The revolution was in full bloom when millions and millions of newly self-created sperm cells went rushing after the egg that clung tenaciously to Taína's inner heavens, and soon, a sperm got there and asked to be let inside. The egg said "yes." The first second of year zero.

And then my vision was over.

I was back on the 6 train.

On my way to school.

It's when I see visions like this one and others like it that I want to hold Taína, smell the shampoo in her hair, and whisper that she and the baby will be fine. That none of this is unreal. For Taína not to worry, because though rare, it is as natural as the fall of apples. Whisper to Taína that the revolution chose you. These rebellious atoms must have seen and felt something pure and kind in you, a body with no chains or kings or gods.

IT WAS TEN p.m. and my mother had finished watching her *novela* and was now listening to the radio as she was getting ready for bed. Sophy sang beautifully:

Locuras tengo por tu nombre / Locuras tengo por tu voz.

I was waiting for her to turn off the radio and go to bed. My mother worked at Mount Sinai's basement doing the hospital's laundry. She was always tired and went to bed early, and my dad was unemployed, so he was a bit depressed and slept a lot. I could easily sneak out of the house at will. El Vejigante had said to meet him at midnight by the mailbox that stood across the street from Taína's window.

All of a sudden Sophy stopped singing, and a news flash about an earthquake in Aracataca, Colombia, came on the radio. Mom shot out of the bathroom, toothbrush in hand,

and listened. The earthquake had triggered massive mudslides, tsunamis of dirt, water, and clay overrunning everything in their path. The voice said people were covered in mud as if God had just created them but had not yet breathed life into them. Rivers of clay were running away with huts and possessions. *"Ay, Dios mío,"* Mom said out loud. The voice continued, saying how people were trying to save their cows from drowning in clay pits. I could hear cows mooing furiously coming through clearly from the radio. The reporter said it was the worst earthquake in Colombia's history, and my mother nodded her head like she knew this was Bible prophecy.

In horror, my mother flicked the radio. I wasn't moving or talking. I lay upside down on the sofa, my head dangling in midair, blood rushing to my brain, and looked up at the clock, hoping Mom would go to bed.

But my mother continued to say these were the "Last Days." She went over to where I was lying and looked down at me. "You have to return to the Truth, Julio. I don't want you to die in Armageddon." From where I lay on the sofa, my mother looked upside down. Blood was running to my head and I felt hot. I could see Mom, but I really couldn't hear her that well.

"¿Me oyes?" She punched my legs, which reached her thighs because I was still lying on the sofa upside down with my head hanging down its edge. "I don't care what happens to that man"—meaning my father, though I knew that was not true—"I love you. *El fin está cerca, Julio.* So *preparate,* Julio," my mom kept saying in Spanish and English.

But I was beyond that. I believed in myself, what I thought was real in me, in my inner heavens. My life was a matter of choices. I was free to make any choice. But I would be held accountable for my choices. So I always tried to choose what was right in my eyes. I no longer went to Mom's church, the Kingdom Hall of Jehovah's Witnesses. Their elders had kicked Taína and her mother out. Yet they still believed in Mary and how she became pregnant while still a virgin. But they did not believe Taína? Why? Because it was not written in some book that isn't even the oldest? The *Gilgamesh* epic is older. So are the *Rigveda* and the *Book of the Dead*. Can a book that is not the oldest book really come from the First All Powerful God? But I respected it because Mom loved it. I respected it because others loved it, too.

"Julio, el fin está cerca." And then my mother began to cry bitterly, like she had been beaten with an iron cord. She knelt down next to me. I quickly sat upright. Blood flowed back down and away from my head, and my mother held me. And I felt embarrassed, even though no one was there, and I embraced my mother, too. And when I saw her face, really, really saw her face, I knew she had been crying before I was born. Such sadness, and maybe it was the reason she loved all those sad songs. While crying, she blamed my father for not helping enough. She blamed him for always being unemployed, and with sobs the words came out as though a dam inside had broken.

"*Pa'* Lincoln"—her tears streaming—"*otra vez pa'* Lincoln, if you keep believing a girl can get pregnant all by herself."

I held my mother tight. She wiped her tears with the back of her hand. I helped her with my own palms, and I felt that she and my father had made me.

"Está bien," she said, crying only a little bit because she had composed herself. *"Sólo prometeme,"* she said, looking straight into my eyes, "that you will stop trying to see that girl, promise me. Those women are trouble." I looked into my mother's eyes. I saw she had worked hard all her life. How she was the only one working right now, keeping us afloat.

"I will not see Taína," I said. My mother nodded, and feeling secured, she wiped her runny nose and went to bed.

Verse 3

AT MIDNIGHT I was outside.

The roundness of the moon, like Taína's stomach, was in full glory. It was a huge yellow moon, its glow bouncing off the project's walls like a tennis ball. My blood was running smoothly; it was not racing with any anticipation of what el Vejigante was going to tell me. I was feeling at peace, as if this were only natural. I felt a light breeze and I leaned on the mailbox. I looked at Taína's window across the street and waited for el Vejigante. I waited past midnight after most of the project's windows went black; even the low glow of Taína's window went silent.

I waited.

And waited.

The first thing I noticed was his shadow on the concrete. It was long and the lamppost's light stretched his silhouette like a noodle. I saw him about a block away and he held not a crowbar but a cane. His cape fluttered because he walked fast, like he was in a hurry. I straightened up and was not afraid. I waited for el Vejigante to reach me, but he crossed the street and entered our project. I knew he was going to visit the two women. My heart was happy because I was sure I was going to be asked up. Or maybe el Vejigante was going to walk out with both Taína and her mother and invite me to walk with them? I happily waited and waited and waited to see for myself if it was true that Taína, like some wonderful mysterious bird, flew only at night.

THERE ARE TIMES when you fall asleep and don't even know it. You wake up and you don't know where you are anymore. I had faded and it was really late. The sky was purple, the way it is right before the sun comes out. I was not upset at el Vejigante for leaving me hanging. I just needed to rush home before my mother woke up to go to her job at Mount Sinai's laundry. I was about to cross the street and go home when I saw el Vejigante walk out of my project. He saw me across the street by the mailbox and smiled just a tad, crossed the street, and walked over to me.

"You're really, really, really late," I said, though I was still happy to see him.

"I knew you were here, *papo,*" he said. "I just needed to be sure."

"Sure of what?"

"Sure that you would wait."

"Are you going to tell Taína about me?"

"I already did," he said. "They are waiting for you."

I inhaled excitedly. I repeatedly thanked el Vejigante. I was ready to cross the street and enter the project. Knock at their door, this early or late, I was going to knock. I did not care about Mom or anything that minute.

"Wait, you can't go up there, *papo*."

"But you just said—"

"You see, *papo,* there's always a price."

And at that moment I realized he held aces up his sleeve. I saw in his eyes a con. El Vejigante was holding on to something. I became distrustful and a bit scared of this old man. He had been bargaining all his life, cutting corners and looking for ways in which he could get something out of people.

"Did you really do all that?" I asked him.

"Do what, *papo*?" He changed his stance; his body was now blocking the lamppost and it added a dark glow to his fading cape.

"What the newspapers said you did," I said.

"When?"

"A long time ago," I said. "You said something about not caring if you burned, and that your mother could watch. You said that when they called you the Capeman."

"How"—he was taken aback, like this was not something he was ready to talk about—"how you know all that?"

"Googled you," I said.

"Oh, yeah. Those things," he said, more to himself, as if he were saying that googling didn't exist in his world, or hadn't in his youth.

"Did you?" I noticed he had pale and sickly skin, like someone who had spent long periods in dark places.

"No, *papo,*" he said in an honest tone, "no, that wasn't me. I'm el Vejigante. Just an old man, you know, *papo*."

"Oh." But I knew it was him. He himself had told me he was the Capeman.

"You want Taína's mother to open the door?" He was switching gears because he didn't want to talk about the Capeman. Which was fine with me. "Then you have to visit as a friend. You see, *papo,* all this time you've been coming in as a stranger. You have to come in as a friend."

"I am their friend," I said.

"No, you're a stranger, *papo*."

"No, I'm their friend," I said again, and he shook his head. The sun was coming up and he picked up his stance like he had to race home or he'd dissolve. He gripped his cane tighter; his long, thin fingers wrapped themselves around it like a snake.

"I'm going to tell you how you can come in as a friend. But if I tell you, you must agree to something, okay, *papo*?" He was worried of the incoming light, as if the sun could hurt him. "We have a deal?"

"Agree to what?" I said.

"I'll tell you later. Now, do we have a deal?"

"Yes." Because I would do anything to be a part of Taína's life.

"So, we have a deal?"

"Yes," I said quickly because I had to get home before my mom woke up. "We have a deal," I said. "Tell me."

"Okay." And he tightened the knot on his cape and held his cane closer, as if letting me know that after he told me this he was going to run home. "Taína is looking at us right now," he said. I looked up at her window but saw no silhouette. "She spends her days looking out the window, and guess at what, *papo*?"

"What?"

"At the mailbox, *papo*."

"The mailbox?"

"Yes, *papo*. Taína is looking at the baby's name. All day long what she is reading is the baby's name." And he was now ready to walk away, but first he pointed at the mailbox. "You see, Taína reads in Spanish, *papo*. When you knock at their door, say that Usmaíl sent you. That's the baby's name and they will let you in."

El Vejigante winked at me before his stork legs took him away as daylight was breaking. I read the mailbox in Spanish. Taína spoke only Spanish, so it was as clear as the daylight that was about to break. OOS-MAH-ILL, Taína read the mailbox in Spanish, Usmaíl. When she stared out of her window, she was admiring the name of her unborn child.

Verse 4

TAKING THE 6 train downtown, I took out one of the many library books I had borrowed on pregnancy and birthing. I always thought that labor was like it was in the movies. The woman feels pain and has to have the baby right there and then, no ifs or buts. In movies women have babies in airplanes, taxis, police cars, Starbucks, but the book said it was nothing like that. Labor took time. Labor was all about time. The book said some women went to the Met during labor and stared at paintings. Some watched baseball and some took a walk through Central Park while keeping time on how apart from one another each labor pain was. It was like tracking a storm: you first hear the thunder and start counting until you see the lightning, and then you do it again; soon you know how close you are till the rains come.

When my stop arrived, I put my pregnancy book away. I then met my class by Wall Street. We were on a trip set up by two teachers. Mr. Gordon was really old, with deep wrinkles like they had been cut into his face. He moved slowly and was waiting to retire. He doubled as the guidance counselor and basketball coach. Every year I had tried out for the team. "I can't teach height," he'd say, and cut me. But Ms. Cahill, the science teacher, was young, good-looking, alive, and always sweet. She once took the class to visit Siena College and Cornell University, both in upstate New York, to show us how these universities are not unreachable. Told us that with hard work, a little luck, and staying out of trouble, we could attend them. Ms. Cahill had been present when Taína sang that day in chorus. It was she who said that in Taína's voice everyone saw whom they loved and who loved them back. I wondered, who had Ms. Cahill seen? Who did she love? I knew that I loved Taína, and so I wanted to hear Taína sing. Hear the one I was in love with sing not just to me but to everyone. So that my love would not be a greedy love, like I had seen many couples display in a universe of only the two of them, but rather through Taína's singing, it would be a love shared by all. And if Taína would not love me back, that was okay, it would suck, but it was okay because I could still continue to love her from a distance, the way Mom loves her old songs of dead singers or people who love paintings that were never alive or books or poems or ponds or places.

THE CLASS FIRST entered the Museum of the American Indian. They had all these Indian artifacts, arrowheads, tomahawks, and clothes made of animal skins. Ms. Cahill would lead us all over the place explaining this or that, but most kids talked over her. But Ms. Cahill was so worked up she'd say, "Think about it, there was a time in New York City when

Indians stood right where you are." And someone would say, "Woopy . . . fucken . . . doo." But she never got annoyed because someone always came to her defense: "Ms. Cahill, he's so stupid, pay no mind." And Ms. Cahill would laugh a little and say, "Look down at the ground, Indians sat cross-legged right here and told stories to one another. In New York City before it was New York City. You might want to write about that for your college essay." And most would look down at their feet, though BD and I were all the way in the back.

"Usmaíl?" BD said as he kept looking at Ms. Cahill's legs from a distance; they were long, thin, and tan. "What kinda name is that?"

"It's the United States mail but read in Spanish." And I said that it was el Vejigante who told me.

"Stop lying. Now I know you lying. That Vejigante don't talk to nobody," BD said.

"Talks to me."

"My mom says that man only comes out at night because he's a faggot."

"So what?" I said. "The world is full of homos."

"And he didn't try anything on you?"

"No," I said. "He's okay."

BD was now looking at Ms. Cahill's ass. She wore her dresses tight, and because of the way she walked her nylons would rub against each other. If you looked closely, you could see the runs gliding down behind her legs.

"That dude comes at me," BD said, "I'll unhook my arm and beat him with it like he owes me money."

"He's a nice *vejigante,*" I said. "He could never hurt anyone." Though I knew he had. "BD, I'm gonna knock at Taína's door after school and say who sent me. You wanna come?"

Ms. Cahill and Mr. Gordon wanted everyone to go outside because we were going to walk around and use our imagination by picturing what it was like when Indians walked on Wall Street.

"Why you want me to come with you, Julio? Isn't this what you wanted all along?"

The class stepped outside and BD lit a cigarette as soon as we were out. He handled his fake arm like it was real. BD never looked awkward doing anything.

"I'm scared, man," I said to BD. "I know this is what I want, but I'm scared."

The class walked around Wall Street, running into little crowded back alleys with laid-down cobblestoned streets from the city's past. "There was once a big wall here." Ms. Cahill outstretched her arms. "That's where the name of this street comes from. Isn't that cool? You might want to write about that for your college essay." But no one thought so.

The class turned the corner and ran into an old bar where George Washington drank. By the entrance was a bearded old man standing on a milk crate with a microphone. "As long as our civilization is essentially one of property, of fences, of exclusiveness," he preached, "it will be mocked by delusions. Our riches will leave us sick." And we all walked on by. Ms. Cahill continued leading the class as all the boys trailed her like puppies. The girls worshipped Ms. Cahill, too; they admired her sense of fashion and the way she fixed her hair.

It seemed that the cops from that area knew Ms. Cahill, too. The cops would see her and say, "Hi, Megan." And she'd act as if she were caught by surprise when it was obvious she knew the cop. We'd turn to yet another block and another cop would say, "Megan, Megan, where you've been?" Even detectives in unmarked cars driving by would stop and get out and flirt with her. With cops around, the boys began to tense up. Ms. Cahill noticed this uneasiness, and she nicely told her cop friends that she couldn't talk right now. She thanked them and kept leading us.

Then one of the girls asked, "You into cops, Ms. Cahill?"

And Ms. Cahill answered in a polite tone, "That is none of your biz." And the class kept walking.

"BD, go with me, man," I said.

"That dude gonna be there?" BD said, smoking.

"I don't know, maybe."

"I ain't going."

Ms. Cahill stopped the class in the middle of the sidewalk and looked around. "Picture tepees, fires burning, animal skins drying up in the sun, right here"—she got all worked up—"on what would become Wall Street. The subway not running underneath, but Indians fishing the Hudson River. That river was their supermarket. Some of you might want to write about that for your college essay," she said, spreading her arms all around like she was painting a landscape.

Old Mr. Gordon just followed along, and one of the students teased him, "You were there, right? You must have hunted with Indians, right, Mr. Gordon?" And he would just smile, knowing he was too old for any of this and simply counting his days till retirement.

"Don't be like that," I said, pulling at BD's good arm.

BD jerked it back. "You sure that's a good giant?" BD said, taking a long drag because we were soon going to enter a new building Ms. Cahill wanted us to experience. "I mean if you want to believe Taína is telling the truth"—taking a puff—"that's one thing. But I don't trust that old dude." And then Ms. Cahill made all those who were smoking put out their butts and the entire class entered the New York Stock Exchange.

"All right, I'll tell you all about el Vejigante," I said to BD.

A young white guy with a fancy suit and tie was there to greet us. On the wall was the largest flag of the United States I had ever seen. The guide first led the class to "the pits," where all these people were screaming and running around the floor littered with paper. It smelled bad. BO heaven, like those guys in suits didn't wear deodorant. They sweated a lot but never took off their blazers. Our guide explained what was going on in the pits. I basically thought it came down to a big fish eating a smaller fish, but he had made it sound like it was exciting rocket science.

"You crazy, Julio. That dude killed people!" BD whispered loudly. "And you wanna go?" BD shook his head in disbelief.

"It was a long time ago, BD."

"I don't care how long ago, that dude's a killer."

We were in the back following the guide along with the rest of the class when Mario arrived late. He shoved an *X-Men* comic book inside his back pocket and stood next to BD and me at the back of the class.

"You know what a bartender calls a Mexican who just crossed the desert?" Mario said to BD.

"What?" BD answered, knowing it was going to be nasty.

"A dry Martinez," Mario said, knowing BD's last name was Martinez.

"Yo, I ain't Mexican," BD said. "I'm Dominican."

"You all Latin spic fucks are the same," Mario said.

"Actually," I added nervously, "you being Italian makes you Latin, Mario. I mean you guys were the original Latins." And even BD gave me this stupid look for stating facts in front of a guy who could kick our asses eight ways to Sunday.

"Who asked you, psycho?" And he slapped the back of my neck.

"He don't hear voices," BD said. "He just thinks that girl is right."

"Yeah," Mario said to BD, "how about you hearing this voice . . ." He got closer to BD and whispered loudly, "One day I'm gonna take your arm and throw it in the East River."

Mario then elbowed his way to the front of the class to be closer at ogling Ms. Cahill's ass.

When the tour was over the guide handed each of us a booklet. The front cover had a shiny new nickel taped to it.

“Even in this recession,” the guide said, “people are buying stocks.” And he held up the pamphlet. “So save your pennies.” He slowed his speech to make sure we’d hear and pointed at the coin taped to the cover. “This nickel is your start, kids. A generous gift from us so that you can be on your way.”

Verse 5

I HAD TAKEN a shower and was ironing my best shirt when I heard my mother talking loudly on the phone. She was on the line with someone from Radio WADO, a Spanish station. Mom kept repeating, "'Lamento . . . Lamento . . . Lamento Borincano,'" as a request, and it seemed that the radio station didn't have that song. "No . . . no . . . *sí,* Rafael Hernández." But the person on the other end didn't understand her. I was wearing my best pair of jeans, had dipped a rag in baby oil to shine my shoes, and was ready to go knock at Taína's door.

Mom covered the phone's mouthpiece. "Who's Marc Anthony?" she asked me.

"A singer, Ma," I said, ready to head out.

"No, 'pera." She handed me the phone.

"I have to go, Ma." But she pushed the phone on me. "I'm going to be late for a school play, Ma."

"Ask them to play 'Lamento Borincano,' but not by this Marc Anthony but by Rafael Hernández."

"Fine," I moaned, and held the phone to my ear.

Mom waited.

I asked.

"They only have Marc Anthony's version, Ma."

"*Ay bendito,* how can that be?" She said, "Tell them that Rafael Hernández's version is better. It's the real Puerto Rican anthem."

I told the person on the other end of the line.

Mom waited.

"Ma, the woman says she's Colombian. She could care less."

"¿Colombiana?" my mother said in disbelief, as if Spanish Harlem were still the same place it was when she was a child. You could still hear a lot of Spanish, but it wasn't just from Puerto Rico. It was an eclectic Spanish with different rhythms and tones from all over the Americas. Mom's Spanish Harlem no longer existed, and maybe it was another reason for her loving those old songs and not moving on.

"Ma, she is not *Boricua,*" I said.

"How can she work at Radio WADO and not be *Boricua*?" Mom said to herself.

Then, like an insect squeaking, I heard the woman's voice on the other end of the line, so I placed the phone back up to my ear.

I nodded as if she could see me.

"Ma," I said, once again covering the mouthpiece, "the lady said she just found a version of 'Lamento' by Shakira. Do you want to hear that one?"

"Who's that?" Before I could answer, Mom fanned the air. "Never mind, never mind, I don't want Shakira. I don't want Marc Anthony. I want what I would hear my parents play." Mom stomped like a spoiled brat. "I want to hear 'Lamento Borincano' by Rafael Hernández."

"Lamento Borincano" is a song my mother loved because her parents loved it, and I love it, too, I guess. It's about a peasant in Puerto Rico who happily plans on selling his produce in the city and buying his wife a new dress with the money. But when he gets there, the city is deserted, the market is empty. A depression has hit the island and many Puerto Ricans have left for the mainland. My mom would wait in anticipation for the line *"Qué será de Borinquen mi Dios querido?"*

"Ma, I have to go. I really have to go," I said. Mom suspiciously stared at how I was dressed. I quickly began to make excuses. "It's a special show at school. I don't want people to see me in sneakers. It's a Shakespearean opera," I said, knowing that that Anglo name would scare her and of course Shakespeare never wrote operas.

With a single look, Mom told me not to go anywhere. She took the phone from me. Told the lady on the line that her husband wanted to talk to the manager of Radio WADO.

Mom yelled my father's name. My Ecuadorian father was in the bedroom taking a nap. My dad got up and stumbled into the living room. My mother ordered him to get Radio WADO to play her song because they would respect a man's voice and not a woman's or a boy's.

Then she turned to me.

"Since when do you dress up?"

"It's a special show."

"¿Tú me está diciendo mentira a mi?"

"No, Ma," I said. "I have to go."

She studied my face, her eyes focused in on mine, her shoulders tensed, and her head tilted a bit.

"Ma, I don't want to be late," I said, because I planned on knocking on Taína's door early. "I'll be home before ten," I said.

"You are not going to see those women, right?"

"Ma, I said I wasn't."

"Even if they don't open the door, you are not going there, right?"

"No, Ma."

"That Taína is trouble, Julio. And her mother—"

"I know, Ma. I know. Can I go now?" I said, annoyed.

"That woman is crazy. That Inelda Flores is crazy. I knew her years ago and she was crazy then."

"Yes, yes, yes, I know. You told me," I said.

Mom's shoulders fell, she inhaled and exhaled loudly, hugged me, and kissed my head.

"Okay, have fun," she said.

"Ma," I said, putting on my best smile, "can I have twenty dollars?"

"What!" My mother is cheap. My father says that when Mom wakes up she looks under the bed to see if she's lost sleep.

"¿Tú crees que yo soy un judío buena gente?"

"I did the laundry this week," I bargained.

Truth is, I could have easily stolen money from her because my mother doesn't trust banks. She changes her ones into fives, fives into tens, tens into twenties, and then into hundreds. She then rolls all her single hundreds into neat tubes and hides them inside an old boot in the closet. My dad thinks that this is a crazy idea. A fire would burn all our life savings. Mom says it is safe because the fire would never reach the closet; it's the smoke that kills you and that money doesn't need oxygen.

"*No tengo*. Have a good time." Mom kissed me good-bye again. I was about to head out when my father hung up the phone. All smiles.

"They are going to play it," he said to Mom in Spanish.

"Finally," Mom said, arms in the air. "I can't wait to hear 'Lamento Borincano' sung by Rafael Hernández."

"'Lamento Borincano'?" My father wrinkled his eyebrows. "I requested 'Guayaquil de Mis Amores' by Julio Jaramillo, of Ecuador." And he sat on the couch happily waiting for his song.

IT WAS ONLY eight flights down the elevator to the second floor. I arrived at 2B. I had taken this ride many times and had always come away empty, but that night something was going to happen. I placed my ear to Taína's door as I had done many times. I had never heard anything. But this time, this time I heard what sounded like the crumpling of leaves. The door shook, too, like there was a strong wind behind it. I heard whispers and whispers like the dead were talking. I began to feel light, as if I could float or the hallway were moving. I looked at the peephole to see if anybody was looking out, but I saw no light escaping. I wiped the sweat off my forehead and remained standing there. I had waited for this moment, and now I was scared, as if there were ghosts on the other side.

I didn't know what else to do and so I yelled at the door, "Usmaíl sent me." Then I said it in Spanish: *"Me mandó Usmaíl."* I repeated it again—"*Usmaíl, Usmaíl*"—and soon the locks began to clack. My heart was a mess wanting to stay and also run away like a reckless comet.

Verse 6

THE DOOR OPENED a tiny bit; the chain was still on. A nose and an eye peeked through. The eye scoped me up and down. In Spanish a female voice asked, "Did Sal send you?" I nodded, though he had told me to say that it was Usmaíl. The door closed, the chain was withdrawn, and the door opened only wide enough for me to enter. Doña Flores did not say anything, only invited me in with the simple gesture of opening the door. As I entered, I looked for Taína, but all I could see was a small empty dark hallway. The place smelled of coffee.

Doña Flores led me to the living room, where I was sure to find Taína sitting by the sofa, watching television, reading, or maybe it was Taína who was making coffee? The lights were low and the shades were drawn. The living room was empty except for the shiny, plastic-covered sofa and love seat. There was a table, a picture of fruits hanging on a wall, and nothing else. I thought for sure there would be an old stereo system, a stack of old records, or an iPod connected to a boom box or something. I knew that Doña Flores had been a great singer. That she had been blessed with a great voice, and like Taína, Doña Flores could make people cry. I had pictured her house overflowing with hints of music. But there was nothing but a sterile silence.

Doña Flores motioned for me to sit down. I hoped the sound of wrinkled plastic would echo loudly and Taína would hear that there was company. I sat hard so the plastic shrieked. Nobody showed up and the house felt darker. Doña Flores sat opposite me on the love seat. Her movements were rough, graceless, nothing like I remembered her elegant daughter's. She was barefoot and wearing a long gown. Her graying hair was in a bun, her face oily, sweaty, and wrinkled. I looked for traces of Taína on her face. I searched for Taína's eyes that sparkled like lakes, but all I saw was a woman whose features time had attacked more violently than it had ever attacked my mother's.

Doña Flores then looked at the wall and said in Spanish, "They used to call people who told the future prophets. Now they call them crazy."

"Claro," I agreed, because I wanted to stay there as long as possible in order to see Taína, who must be somewhere.

"Oh, no, I was not talking to you, *mijo,*" she said in Spanish. Like my mother, Doña Flores switched between English and Spanish when it suited her. She said she had felt bad for me standing by that mailbox. Staring up at her window like a dog left out in the rain. "*Bendito,* part of me really wanted to open the window and yell to go home before you get mugged." She laughed a little. "And your mother, how is she?"

"Fine." I looked around the empty living room for traces

of Taína. There was a door that led to a bedroom. If Taína was not sleeping, she must have been hearing us from behind that door.

"Your mother . . ." Doña Flores's face was remembering happy times, I think. "We were once close."

"Yes, I know, Doña," I said.

"I was kicked out of the Truth, so your mother doesn't talk to me anymore." She looked at the wall again and said, "But, *ay bendito,* what can you do, Jehovah." And I didn't make much of it because people who talk to God and walls are one and the same. I mean, neither a wall nor God will talk back. Plus I had my visions, so I lived in that same strange glass house. I could not throw stones at anyone.

"Is Taína home?" I asked politely. Doña Flores got up.

"You want some coffee, *mijo*?"

"Yes." I didn't like coffee but figured it was only a matter of time before Taína would come out. The living room was empty, but I could feel the dust of her dead cells, loose strands of her hair, Taína's prints, all around. I was sitting where she must nap. I was looking at things that she must see and touch. My feet stood where she walked. I could feel Taína's presence. And I was happy.

Doña Flores came back from the kitchen. She held out a mug.

"Thank you." I took the coffee.

"Salvador said that you knew the baby's name."

"Yes," I said, not taking a sip. "Usmaíl."

"You know Salvador is like my Ta-te." She sat down, cup in hand.

"Like Taína?" I said, knowing fully well that Ta-te was her motherly way of calling Taína.

"Yes, both are saints."

"Taína is," I said, because a saint is whom you want to believe in. "I know Taína sings. She sings beautifully. Maybe we can . . ." And I trailed off because Doña Flores made a disgusted face, letting me know she disagreed with me somewhat. I stayed quiet. She took a long sip that told me she was going to talk for a while.

"First, *mijo,*" she said, "Salvador is also a saint. And he doesn't like that he is called el Vejigante, but accepts it because he has suffered. *Dios mío,* has that man suffered. Like all saints he has suffered."

And she slowly guided me through el Vejigante's young life. How much he had suffered, she said. How Salvador was six months old when his father deserted them. His mother checked both into the Casa Isla de Pobres in Mayagüez, Puerto Rico. Salvador's mother worked as a maid for the nuns. They ate together in the same room, mostly boiled potatoes, *plátanos,* and bread, all served in different variations depending on the day. The casa was a place of locked iron doors and wired fences. Of endless dark hallways and the nuns remaining in the silent background. They were women who kept their eyes low and lifted them only when they needed to punish the orphaned children. It was a silent casa of whispers and hisses, a casa where talking was a disturbance. But at night anyone outside could hear the lunatic screams of those who had gone crazy, the suffering of derelicts, the moaning of the dying, and the sobs of lost and forgotten children. When Salvador turned nine, his mother met a Pentecostal pastor who took them away from the casa and to New York City, where a different kind of trouble started for Salvador.

Doña Flores then looked at the wall again but didn't say anything back to what or whom she was seeing. She turned to me again. "What happened later in New York City, when he was about your age, in the playground," she said, following my eyes, which always landed on what I knew must be Taína's bedroom door. "He was just an ignorant kid. Salvador couldn't even read or write like a saint. He was a victim. Just like those kids that night."

"Sure," I said, "he was just a kid." Though I didn't completely agree.

"Like my Ta-te, Salvador has done nothing wrong."

"How do you know?" I said, no longer staring at Taína's door. It had taken me all this time to realize that Taína would not come out. Doña Flores was hiding her from me. Her tone told me she knew what I wanted, but I had to give her something first. I did not know what that was. She was telling me things about el Vejigante's past in order to study me. To see my expressions and draw her conclusion. Doña Flores must have noticed me shaking. I had been dreaming of seeing Taína for what seemed like forever, and all I had was the outside of her bedroom door.

"I knew you were there," she said.

"Where?"

"At night, behind us, following us. Salvador did, too. You know he only comes out at night." She held my eyes. "You want to see my daughter?" Slowly nodding like she knew a secret she was not going to tell me. "You want to see Ta-te, huh?"

"I do." As if saying it would make her tell Taína to come out.

"You want to hear my Ta-te sing?"

"Yes," I repeated excitedly. And I told Doña Flores what I could not say to anyone, but I knew it was true. "I think I love her."

Doña Flores did not laugh. She did not say, What do you know about love, you're just a kid? What are you going to feed the baby, snow? You can't even sleep without drooling and you are in love? She never said anything like that, which was what my mother would have said. Instead Doña Flores straightened her head, put her coffee down, crossed her arms, looked at the wall again.

"I want to talk to her," I said, "tell her what has happened to her body, very, very deep inside her body."

"What, *mijo*?" She turned her face to one side, showing me only her profile, half lips, one eye, reading me, searching for something.

"A revolution," I said.

"A revolution?"

I told her what I was sure had happened in an inner space world full of electricity. I did my best to describe to Doña Flores the quantum world I had read in books and seen on TV shows and studied in science class, a world riddled with paradoxes and other dimensions. How inner space doesn't follow the same rules as those of our big universe. The things that exist in inner space are not tied down to one location or definition. Atoms, which I told her make up everything, live in an inner universe that doesn't follow the same rules we do. Gravity has no power in their world, neither does light nor speed. I said atoms might even have their own gods. The inner universe belonging to Taína's body is where Usmaíl is from.

"There was a war in her body—"

Doña Flores cut me off by laughing.

Laughing and laughing. This from a woman who talked to walls, but it was okay.

"Taína needs an ultrasound," I said, changing the gears, "to make sure the baby is healthy, to check the spine, and Taína needs a Lamaze class for exercise, and she needs—"

"I gave birth without any of those things, *mijo,*" she said, a bit annoyed. I dropped it because I wanted to be invited back.

She whispered something to the wall again. She waited for an answer and I guess got one.

"*Sólo* Peta Ponce," she said to me. "Peta Ponce can bring the truth out. What happened to Ta-te. What happened to Ta-te, *sólo* Peta Ponce *puede.*"

"Who?" I said, but she got up and took my coffee cup away. She was going to kick me out soon.

"Peta Ponce. Peta Ponce can make my Ta-te sing again. If you want to see Ta-te," she said, "Salvador said you could do this."

"Do what?" I said.

She sucked her teeth, followed by a loud sigh. "Look around, Juan Bobo." She called me the Puerto Rican name of the village idiot. I looked around but saw nothing but an empty dark living room. Doña Flores rolled her eyes. "Salvador said you could get us the money so we can bring Peta Ponce here. *Comprendes,* Juan Bobo?"

At that instant I heard the bathroom's door open slightly. I stood up and looked toward the bathroom. A skinny ray of light shot through, landing on the floor like someone had taken chalk and drawn a yellow line. The line became fatter and through the half-open door I saw Taína. She was wearing a moth-eaten see-through gown. I had never known there was a tiny dark brown mole on her left thigh. With awe I shivered at how her stomach was full, her breasts swollen. I could feel my heart beating. I did not hear music, but I saw circles that made circles that crashed into moons and stars. I saw all these colors, like I had been punched in the eye, triggering fireworks inside my irises. It must have been only seconds, but my eyes managed to take in every detail. Taína turned her head, caught me standing there, ogling at her like a dork. *"¡Qué carajo mira, puñeta! ¿Qué? ¿Nunca ha' visto chocha?"* She slammed the door shut.

Verse 7

IT WAS NOT hard finding out where el Vejigante lived. In El Barrio, many had heard about a tall old man who came out only at night. All I had to do was ask around. Soon, I arrived at one of the few remaining walk-ups on 120th and First Avenue. I knocked at the basement's door, which unlike Doña Flores's opened quickly. El Vejigante was in shorts, wearing a T-shirt that read: *PA'LANTE, SIEMPRE PA'LANTE*. He had black socks and was eating a bowl of cornflakes. A skinny old man eating away and happy to see me.

He held the bowl with one hand and shaded his eyes from the light with the other.

"Hey, *papo,* come in. Come in. Thank you for visiting this *viejo*."

The place was a phenomenal dark dump. "You want a knife? A crowbar? I got a baseball bat—"

"No, Salvador." I called him by his real name because all the stuff he had done was so long ago. "I trust you and you know what I'm here for." Everything in his tiny basement apartment was fading. The floors were slanted and there were only two windows facing the street above, where you could see the feet of people walking by. The place had a nice lavender smell, though, like some botanicas. A short hall connected the kitchen to the living room, and stacked against one wall were all these books and broken television sets without plugs or knobs. The sets were piled on top of one another and were not dusty, like he must be cleaning them with Windex every day. There was a broken-down sofa and pictures of Puerto Rican landscapes hanging on the walls. But it was the curtains with pictures of kittens, flowers, and saints that told me this was once his mother's house.

"Hey, you want some beans?" He put his bowl down, took two steps to the kitchen, and showed me government-issued cans.

"Nah, it's okay."

"Hey, I got cheese, I got powdered milk, I can add water and get you a bowl of cornflakes? I got . . . ? I got . . . ? Ham, I can make you a sandwich."

"No, I'm good." He had been in prison for years; he must have always been hungry. So I figured he thought everyone else must be hungry, too.

His tiny apartment must have been as big as a whale's mouth compared with a cell. But it was way better than living with rats and roaches and bedbugs for roommates in a place where lights went out at the same hour. An old wooden piano that took up most of the space stood against a wall, its ivory keys as yellowed as an old man's teeth.

"You play that?" I asked, pointing at the piano.

"Sometimes," he said. "You know, music runs in the

family," he said happily, and put the cans down. "You wanna hear something, *papo*? I can play you something. It's not in tone, the F key and the E key get stuck, you know, ruins the flats and the sharps, but the rest work well, you know, *papo*? You wanna hear me play?"

"You know why I'm here," I said, though I wanted to hear him play.

"The thing about money, right?"

"Yeah, how can you tell them I could get them money when I'm still in school?" I said. "And what does that make Taína's mother? Saying I have to pay to see her daughter?"

The jewel in his basement apartment was a bright red, white, and yellow *vejigante* costume. It hung by the closet door like another person was there with us. I recalled that I had seen that same costume in last year's Puerto Rican Day Parade because it had the same political button pinned to it, *¡Puerto Rico Libre!*

"I didn't lie to you, *papo*." Salvador sat down on the musty sofa, his knees almost touching his chest.

"Yes, you lied. I know because I lie to my parents all the time." I stayed standing, looking at the *vejigante* costume. The cape and suit were made from the same colorful fabric, while the large mask with horns, lots of horns coming out from all sides, was papier-mâché. I could have sworn the costume moved.

"*Mira, papo,* I know those women because Inelda is my half-sister."

"Taína is—"

"My niece, yeah, that's how it works, *papo*."

"What's Taína like?" I excitedly asked him.

"She's a kid. She's like you."

"Yeah, okay. But what does she like, you know, like to eat?"

"Same things you like to eat."

"I like pizza." I shrugged.

"Then Taína likes pizza, too."

"Okay."

"Listen, *papo,* all my sister wants is just a few hundred bucks here and there to cover what her welfare check can't. Know what I'm saying, *papo*?" He looked embarrassed, as if he were asking for my forgiveness or that he wasn't worthy of anyone's attention. "What Inelda wants is a really nice bed because her back hurts and a television because she likes to watch *novelas*. But more than anything, what my sister wants is to have this famous *espiritista* from Puerto Rico come to her house and you can't pay an *espiritista* with WIC checks."

"Peta Ponce?"

"That's her. Peta Ponce is known all over and she costs a lot of money. She's the real thing."

"What you mean?"

"Peta Ponce"—and he crossed himself—"has the power to confuse time. The spirits tell her everything, they lend her the power to twist and transform feelings. You know, bend sadness to happiness, curl shame into love."

"Wow, sounds weird."

"No, it's serious stuff, *papo*. Inelda knows her, and so does your— You sure you don't want any food?" he said, walking two steps to the small old refrigerator, which he opened, looked into as if he were proud and happy that he had food, and then closed.

"How does Doña Flores know this *espiritista*?"

He sat back down, took a deep sigh like he needed it.

"Peta Ponce helped my sister after her pregnancy . . . and your . . ." He licked his lips and changed his mind. He kept catching and stopping himself. So I asked again.

"My what?" I said. "My what, Sal?"

But silence fell.

I waited.

I stared at his *vejigante* costume, his only connection to daylight.

The first time anyone had seen Salvador was during last year's Puerto Rican Day Parade. He was marching wearing this costume. He was so tall he didn't need stilts. He marched gracefully and fluidly. This natural, elegant, nimble *vejigante* would march close to the stands where the people were cheering on the parade, waving Puerto Rican flags. People thought it was a young guy inside that costume. But after the parade was over, Sal took off his *vejigante* mask and they saw an old man. They all laughed and Salvador didn't mind one bit, he laughed with the people. The next thing you know, he became a staple in the neighborhood, another eccentric of El Barrio who kept to himself and came out only at night. No one knew about his past. Only I knew, and that was because he had wanted me to know.

"Can't you just introduce me to Taína? You know I wanna help," I said.

"I can't, *papo*."

I was happy we were talking again.

"Why?"

"Because you, *papo,* are the only one who can get my sister money to bring the *espiritista* to New York," he said.

"She has you," I said.

"Me? Look at me," he said, without a trace of sadness or regret, like he had accepted the cards that had been dealt to him. "I'm old. I'm old and living in my mother's place, the rent is paid by what's left of her Social Security. I eat what Uncle Sam gives out through churches. Inelda"—he always called Doña Flores by her first name—"isn't doing much better than me and she has a daughter who's pregnant. You all she has, *papo*. You it."

As broke as my parents were, there was always food and stuff. Even when my father lost job after job, we didn't go on welfare. My mother had vowed never to go on welfare. She had always been a proud workingwoman that never had taken a dime from the government. If anything, the government took a lot from her check. But Doña Flores, Taína, and Salvador were *pegaó* at the bottom of the pot.

"Okay," I said, "but how much she needs?"

"A hundred dollars here and there, *papo*. To buy stuff for the baby, get the place ready before the baby arrives." But for me a hundred dollars here and there was a lot. "And five thousand for the *espiritista*."

"You crazy!" My eyebrows shot up. "Five thousand! No way can I get that. There is no way I can get that."

"Don't panic, *papo*. I'm going to show you how. It's a way to take care of yourself."

"Okay, how?" I said. "You gonna get me a job?"

"No," he said.

Just then the costume that was hanging by the closet door fell to the floor. It collapsed onto itself as if it were a skinny man who had lost his skeleton all of a sudden and just crumpled. Only the colorful horned mask stayed hanging, because a nail above the door was holding the mask.

"That hanger is bent," Salvador said, "it falls all the time." And he went over to pick up his costume. "The *vejigante* came from twelfth-century Spain, you know, *papo*? Saint James defeated the Moors, and see, *papo*"—and he began to inspect his costume and brushed some dust away—"in Spain the *vejigantes* represented the Moors. The *vejigantes* terrified the people, so their only salvation was the Catholic Church or facing the Muslims. When the Spaniards conquered Puerto Rico, we inherited their demon," he said, "but we embraced the Muslims. We put the Muslims in our parades, we turned the *vejigante* from something horrific into something pretty great." And he hooked his costume back on the hanger.

"You're very smart," I said. "Why did you kill those kids?"

And silence fell again.

Salvador did not like my question. When he had greeted me, he was like a kid, and now he looked haggard and gaunt like the old man that he was.

"Sorry about that, *papo*." He meekly hunched his timid shoulders. Spit gathered at the corner of his mouth. "I forgot what you had come here for."

"It's okay," I said, "I got to go." I felt stupid for asking him again about that night at the playground. I was tripping him into telling me something he didn't want to talk about. There was no law that said he had to tell me anything. He had spent years in prison and had done his time. And I felt really, really stupid, too, because there was no way I could get a hundred dollars here and there, let alone five thousand for this *espiritista* so that Doña Flores would let me see Taína. I knew where my mother hid her money and I planned on stealing it.

"It's not your fault," I said. "I just want to help Taína, that's all."

"*Papo,* I can show you how to get the money. It's a scam. I'm old, but when I was your age, when I was"—and he paused but said it again—"the Capeman, I would run it myself." He stared at me like he did when we first met, weighing in on if he should tell me anything. His hazel eyes were hard and weary, like he had seen the death of love.

"I only go out at night, *papo* . . . ," he said in a docile tone. He had gone to a place that made him regretful. "The daytime . . ." His face was a flood of tears with no weeping sounds. He sat back on the couch and hid his wet face with his hands. "After what I did that night," he said, his voice muffled through his palms. "I only go out at night, *papo,* because the daylight, *papo* . . . it shames me. The light shames me."

THE THIRD BOOK OF JULIO

DOG DAYS

I have no recollections in detail but I have vague and great subconscious feelings that terrible things took place, things that no one alive, mentally awake, could bear to see, much less experience.

—FELIPE ALFAU, *LOCOS*

Verse 1

SPANISH HARLEM AND the Upper East Side live next door to each other like the prince and the pauper. The Upper East Side's Fifth Avenue being the Gold Coast. Its streets are aligned with elegant doorman buildings, with movers and shakers and movie stars living in them. Central Park is their backyard. Spanish Harlem is another story. Full of projects, old tenements, and these new but cheaply made expensive rentals where the mostly white young professional new residents live. I could easily walk downtown from my project building on 100th Street and First Avenue and go from dirt poor to filthy rich in ten minutes. I'd walk down Fifth Avenue and see young white girls in summer dresses. Young white boys my age in khakis, white shirts, and blazers with the school's crest patched on the breast pocket. I'd dream of living their lives. In their buildings, in their neighborhoods, with maybe Taína and the baby at my side. I wanted to know where they were going. What doorman building did they call home? What working elevator carried them to high and wonderful views of this city?

Hunting was what Salvador called it. He said that it was okay because we were not hurting anything or anyone and those rich people living on Park or Fifth Avenue were old-money people. They had money to burn, and most likely their grandparents or great-grandparents had destroyed lives, killed some part of the planet, in order to acquire their wealth. All I was doing was taking a little bit back from what once belonged to "the people" whom the city was not taking care of and so we had to fend for ourselves.

And I wanted Doña Flores to let me visit again.

"You want to go hunting?" I asked BD.

"Fuck's that?" he said, knowing it wasn't really what it sounded like.

"We take a laundry bag, okay, and a knife and pace the streets of the Upper East Side on the lookout for a lapdog that's leashed to a lamppost or something, while the owner is inside somewhere drinking coffee or something." I said it exactly the way Salvador had explained it to me. "Outside beauty salons are good, so are cafés, and post offices are good, too."

"So?" BD shrugged his shoulders.

"We unleash the dog or cut the leather leash and stuff the small dog in the laundry bag and run," I said. BD took out a Jolly Rancher with his real arm and starting sucking on it. He didn't give me one. "I take the dog home, feed it, walk it, and groom it. Two or three days later, you and me go comb the same streets where we took the dog and look for the reward flyers." When BD heard this he stopped sucking his Jolly Rancher and his face lit up, his tongue blue like the sky.

"Yo, that's crazy. Will it work?"

"Of course it'll work. Those people love their dogs."

"Dogs bite, Julio. I don't know."

"We ain't gonna take a German shepherd. A lapdog, stupid."

"How much can we get?"

I was happy BD had agreed. "I don't know. Five hundred, three hundred and fifty dollars a dog, maybe?"

BD liked that idea.

"Okay," I said, "but you know my mom or anyone can't ever find out."

"Who am I going to tell? The cops?" Like it was stupid of me to have even mentioned it. "Hey, so how it turned out the other day, did you see that bitch?"

"Come on, BD." I made a face.

"All right, all right." He took out a Jolly Rancher and gave it to me. "Did you see Taína?"

"A little bit."

"Did she talk?"

"She cursed."

"Did she sing?"

"No. But she will."

"I think you crazy. She can't get pregnant without someone jamming her."

"Then why," I said, rolling my candy to the side of my mouth, "do you go with your mother to church every Sunday?"

"I told you, God is a man, and like all dudes he likes to jam girls, too. Why is it hard for you to understand that?"

"Never mind," I said. "So you in on this, right?"

"Yeah, sounds like fun." BD nodded. "I'm in."

"All right. But wait, there is more."

"Yeah, yeah, more money?" BD said, as if he were already thinking what he was going to buy with his share.

"We're gonna need your little brother, Ralphy."

BD AND I did exactly what Salvador had instructed me to do. We combed the wealthy streets of the Upper East Side on the lookout for a lapdog that was left outside unattended. When we found this cute little black dog outside a Victoria's Secret on 86th Street and Third Avenue, BD cut the leash. I grabbed the dog and we ran.

LATER AT HOME.

"Whose dog is that?" my father asked in Spanish.

Salvador had told me exactly what to say to my parents.

"I got a job as a dog sitter," I said in English, because my father does understand English; he just doesn't like to speak it. I gave the dog water and fed it. Then my mother walked in from work.

"Look," my father told her in Spanish, "Julio has a found a job. I cannot find a job, but my son has found a job."

"Job? What job?" Mom took off her shoes, the first thing she always does. She had that day's mail in hand. There was a letter from Lincoln Hospital. I was glad when she didn't open it and just dropped the entire mail on the table. "Whose dog is that? It's cute," she said, and then turned the radio on low volume.

"I'm babysitting dogs while their owners are on vacation," I said in English, because Mom talks in both depending on her mood and sometimes mixes the languages.

"You don't babysit dogs, you babysit babies," Mom said. "How much they are paying you?"

I gave them the number that Salvador had said they would usually ask for.

"About five hundred dollars!"

My father whistled to himself. Leonardo Favio sang on the wire.

"I don't believe this," Mom said, humming just a bit to the melody. "You have a job, really happy. Good."

"Ma, those rich *blanquitos* on the Upper East Side love their dogs, so they rather pay me to take care of it than to put it in a kennel for days. So they pay me."

"Está bien." Then Mom finally kissed the top of my head hello.

Pops got ready to serve us dinner. My father always cooked, but he never served. This began years ago when my mother was cleaning and Pops offered to help. Pops did such a bad job washing dishes that Mom had to do them over again. So she said to him, "The best way a man can help a woman is by not doing anything at all." My father didn't like that and he said, "From now on I will cook, but you will have to serve yourself." And once even right before dinner, when my parents thought I wasn't listening, I heard my father say to her in Spanish, "I want you to serve me with your work uniform on." Mom said she did hospital laundry and was not a French maid. My father then said that he had taken one of her uniforms from the closet and cut it up a certain way and that he wanted his dinner served with her wearing that. And by some miracle, Mom gave me five dollars that day and told me to go outside and get pizza so they can be alone. So that's how it's been, my Ecuadorian father cooks but my Puerto Rican mother serves the food.

"Now that you work you can help me with the bills," Mom said, getting the dishes ready and placing them on the table and humming to Leonardo Favio on the radio. They both sang about a woman who might one day hear a song and be enraptured by it, and she will cry but won't be able to go back in time, back to that affair.

Pops had made rice and beans and what smelled like *chuletas*. "You know it better not bark too loud and wake me." Mom placed the dishes on the table.

"I just have to feed it and walk it three times a day for three days, Ma." Because Salvador had told me it takes about that long before the owner has gone through all venues like the ASPCA and the cops to finally posting reward flyers. "I'll keep the dog in my room and walk it before and after school and feed it. No problems."

" 'Tá lindo," Mom said, looking at the dog, who barked in the cutest way.

"This is the most wasteful country." My father sat at the dinner table, shaking his head in disbelief. "In Ecuador who would imagine paying a kid to take care of a dog."

"Shut up, Silvio," Mom said. "Thank Jehovah your son has a job."

"What a wasteful country," my father said again.

No puedo enfrentar esta realidad / De no verte más, de mi soledad . . .

"Did I tell you what your father did when we first got married?"

"Yes, many times," I said, though I knew she'd tell it again.

"Your father goes to the supermarket and comes back all happy, saying he found a bargain. Your father says, 'I bought us ten cans of tuna for a dollar. Ten cans of tuna, we'll save money and eat tuna for a week.'" She tried hard not to laugh. "And I tell him, 'You dummy, that's cat food.'"

"What did I know?" my father defended himself. "What did I know? I had been in this country for only a few weeks! I did not think that people bought cats food. In Ecuador, who would buy a cat food? The cat eats what you throw away." But my mother was laughing up a storm and the dog liked it because he jumped on her lap and began to bark at her for attention. The dog seemed not to miss his owner as long as he was fed, walked, and loved.

"Didn't the picture of the cat on the can tell you something?" Mom laughed harder.

"I thought that was the brand." Pops shrugged. "At least Ecuador is not a colony of the United States, we are our own country."

"Don't start that," Mom said, annoyed, and raised the volume of the radio so that Leonardo Favio could drown out Pops instead of her.

"I'll be back in ten." And I leashed the dog.

My father, hearing that I was leaving, went over to the

radio and turned it down into a whisper and in an apologetic low tone, asked Mom, "Are you going to serve me dinner wearing your laundry uniform?" I took a deep breath and went to walk the little dog that was going to bring me closer to Taína as my mother went to get changed, singing.

Verse 2

I WOKE UP, yawned, and grabbed myself with such a natural security. The first image of the day that entered my mind was Taína singing in the shower. I was happy. Smiling, I pictured Taína's stomach, how the shampoo's foam slid off her wet body. I was not there. I was not doing anything to Taína. I simply saw the image of her naked body on the ceiling as I lay flat on my bed. It was like a white shadow similar to the images of her looking out her window. Then I thought about the few times I had heard her voice, and it seemed as if she were there in my room, singing. Electricity exploded inside me. A stunning display of sparks skidded upward. I felt no shame or regret. I got up, found a sock on the floor, and wiped myself clean. When I went to get some clean clothes, I slid the drawer and there in plain sight was a *Watchtower* magazine. The title had to do with drugs and how they affect the mind. I knew my mother had planted it there for me. In our conversations, neither Mom nor Pops had the courage to ask me if I was doing any drugs. I was only smoking pot with BD and not even regularly. I had few friends, and those that spoke to me were not the ones that were cool enough to smoke. I didn't plan on reading *The Watchtower*. I did open the magazine, making sure that its spine got creased, so hopefully my mother would think that I had read it.

AT THE SCHOOL entrance two white guys wearing jewelry and with too much bass on their radio parked by the curb. They turned the engine off but not the booming radio. One of them got out of the car, gold chains slapping his chest as he bopped and weaved like he was shadowboxing. It was Mario, and he was coming straight at me. I took my eyes away from the car to look at anything else but him. I waited for the slap or the insult, but he walked past me as if he were too cool to pick on me. This was fine with me.

Ms. Cahill started her class by handing out old science textbooks that smelled like milk from a cow whose insides were fading. She noticed everyone wrinkling their noses. Ms. Cahill was disgusted, too.

"I know these are a bit old, but they were the best books I could find."

"Yo, like these books are so old, Ms. Cahill," someone called out, "they knew Burger King when he was a prince."

The class laughed.

"Central Park when it was a plant," someone joined in.

The class laughed louder.

"Shut up," someone shouted.

"You shut up."

"No, you shut up."

"No, you whose mother is so poor, she went to McDonald's to put a Big Mac on layaway."

Now it was a free-for-all.

"Yeah? Well, your mother is so poor, she sewed rubber pockets to your coat so you can steal soup."

"Please, girlfriend. When your Dominican mother hears the weatherman say, 'It's chilly outside,' she sends you out with a bowl."

Ms. Cahill did her best to restore order, but sometimes, when she found the snaps funny, she couldn't help laughing. So the chaos continued.

"Well, your mother thinks 'menopause' is a button on the DVD player."

"Yours thinks 'manual labor' is the president of Panama."

"Yours thinks 'illegitimate' means you can't read."

Ms. Cahill stopped laughing and said, "Okay, enough, enough."

"Well, your mother is so fat and stupid, she tore up your computer looking for cookies."

"Enough"—though Ms. Cahill was laughing again at full speed—"enough."

"Yeah, well, your mother is so stupid, she got fired from a blow job."

"Yeah, well, you know the difference between a joke and ten black guys? Your mother can't take a joke."

"Enough!" Ms. Cahill stopped laughing. She bit her cheeks so she wouldn't laugh again. "I hate it as much as you," she said in that sweet and lovely voice of hers, "but some of the material in these books can still be used."

"Yeah, for wrapping fish," Mario said, drinking a Yoo-hoo milk drink and reading a comic book.

"Listen!" Ms. Cahill was now annoyed and she looked at Mario. "Let's not start these jokes again, okay?" The class quieted down.

"Chemistry is about life. . . ." Ms. Cahill began her lesson. "Electrons change their orbits, molecules change their bonds. Elements combine and change their compounds. That's life right there. Change. Life and death and life again. All happening in a place so small we can never really see, much less visit, but know what is happening there."

I was happy when I saw BD out by the classroom door, waving. I raised my hand and asked for permission to go to the bathroom. Ms. Cahill gave it after she said she needed to talk to me about my college essay. I nodded and took the pass and met BD out by the hallway.

"Yo, I found it, I found it." He gave me the flyer. I was surprised, because it had been only two days and Salvador had said it took about three or four for the dog owners to put up flyers. I read the flyer and it was our dog.

REWARD FOR LOST DOG.

Last seen on 86th Street and Third Avenue.

If you've seen my pet, please contact L. Sloan at

212-555-8612. Reacts to the name Cosmo.

"And check it out, see, it was last seen on the same block, near the Victoria's Secret where we stole it. No doubt, Julio, it's the same dog," BD said.

"We didn't steal it," I said. "We are borrowing it."

"If that's what you need to tell yourself. I just want the money," BD said.

"Don't forget Ralphy." I folded the flyer and put it in my back pocket.

AT HOME I took the dog for a walk and fed it. I got dressed up, combed my hair, and shined my shoes with baby oil. I then met BD and his six-year-old brother, Ralphy, the cutest little kid ever, outside my project. I made the call from a pay phone. I knew words held power and for some reason practiced saying the word "aimlessly" as best as I could sounding like a white kid. So when the person on the other line picked up, I said, "Lady, I think we have found your dog, he was walking aim-less-ly in Central Park."

"Are you sure it's my Cosmo?" A woman's voice was overjoyed.

"Yes, is that his name?" As if I didn't know. "We can bring him over."

THOUGH WE ALREADY knew it from the flyer, she gave us her address. And we took off for the Upper East Side. We arrived and the doorman called the lady from a phone in the lobby and she said to send us up. The elevator walls were all brass, though they looked like gold, and the smell of piss or beer was nowhere to be found. Riding up in the elevator, BD told his little brother to cry. Ralphy, who held the little dog in his arms, cried like he was headed toward the dentist. The elevator let us off right into her apartment. I thought it was amazing, an elevator inside your house.

"Lady, is this your dog? My little brother here loves him, but when we found out he was lost, we brought him back," I said, and the young, very pretty white lady's face was aglow. She inhaled loudly and reached to take her dog from little Ralphy, who held on to it tighter and continued to cry his eyes out.

"I'll get you another one, one that looks just like that one," I said to Ralphy.

"Yeah, Ralphy, come on, we'll get you another dog. This one is the lady's," BD said to his little brother.

"It's my dog, Ralphy," she said, calling BD's little brother by his name as if she knew him. "I'm sorry, but it's my dog, Ralphy." Her face had fallen. She sweetly and sadly knelt down to take the dog. Ralphy let go of the dog, who quickly jumped on the lady like she was his mother. The lady had a jeweled necklace dangling from her neck like Saturn. Her nails were really sparkling and her teeth were dove white. She cooed at her dog, who returned her love with a laughing bark.

"Bye," I said, as Ralphy buried his crying face in BD's arms.

On cue, BD's fake arm fell off. It made a loud noise as it hit her polished wooden floors. The young lady gasped like she was out of breath, and she covered her mouth in horror. Without any inconvenience, BD picked his arm back up, relocated it, and then held his crying little brother and said, "Let's go, fellas."

"Wait!" the lady cried out, as if she had done us a disservice. "There is a reward."

OUTSIDE. ON PARK Avenue we turned the corner and started running. We would have continued maybe all the way back to Spanish Harlem, all the way back to 100th Street and First Avenue, except that Ralphy was too little and he got tired.

"You said you were going to buy me a hundred penny candies if I cried." Ralphy was upset at his big brother.

"I am," BD said, and gave him a Jolly Rancher. We were in the street, and I wasn't going to take out money. So we went inside a pizzeria, ordered pizza and Cokes, and sat all the way in the back. I began to count. It was a lot of money, and I could almost see Doña Flores's happy, smiling face.

Verse 3

EARLIER, I HAD arrived with two bags of groceries, Pampers, talc, wipes, blankets, Cokes, a manicure set, Q-tips, chewing gum, Blow Pops, Lemonheads, Nerds, Kit Kats, and a lot of junk food because I had read in the books I had borrowed from the library that pregnant women ate a lot of junk food. I knocked and waited. I then realized that Doña Flores was not going to open unless I slipped the envelope with money under her door. So I did. I soon heard the sound of bills being counted, the whispering of numbers in Spanish. Only then did the locks clack, and she opened the door only wide enough for me to enter sideways with the bag of groceries.

Doña Flores's face was pleased. She spoke to the wall in a very surprised Spanish, "Juan Bobo did it." I corrected her that my name was Julio. She nodded, but I knew she was laughing at me. Laughing at me with the walls she talked to. But I didn't really care. I could hear my heartbeat doing those circles around circles and retracing those same circles because I was soon going to see Taína.

I had told Doña Flores that I was in love with her daughter, and though I was sure, I didn't know how to tell Taína this. I was also afraid of her potty mouth.

I walked inside and Doña Flores stacked the cartons of diapers on one side of the empty hallway. In the living room, Doña Flores motioned for me to wait. With one hand she held the money, and some of the groceries with the other. She knocked at Taína's door and said, "Ta-te." And the circles in my heart were now forming other shapes and figures, floating, wiggling, and bouncing inside me like some abstract painting and all I could do was look at the floor.

"¿Tú eres Julio?" Taína said in a Spanish that sounded delicate. "That's a pretty dumb, stupid fucking name." She switched to English: "The dumbest, ugliest shit name I have ever heard." But it made me happy she thought my name was pretty dumb and stupid. "You shouldn't look at people when they are in the fucking bathroom," she scolded me with the tone of a command.

"Yeah, yeah, I'm sorry. I was just there," I answered, looking at the floor. I would have smiled at Taína, but I wasn't able to look up. I was scared to be blinded in some nervous way. I simply looked at Taína's *chancletas*. They were a plastic orange. All her ten toes showed chipped remnants of cherry-red nail polish, and there was a big Snoopy Band-Aid taped across her big toe. When I did look up, a thin cotton blue-gray see-through gown the color of a seagull's eye covered her pregnant body. The gown was wrinkled, as if she had slept in it. It was hard not to pay attention to those places that boys are not supposed to stare at. And so I kept my head down.

"Do you like pizza?" I said, looking not at her but rather at Doña Flores, who was putting away the groceries. "You know pizza?"

"Pizza?"

"Pizza, to eat?" I said, and tried not to smile too much. To not look at her see-through gown, though she must have known that her brown nipples were poking out as if they, too, were making fun of me. "Pizza, it has cheese and stuff."

"I know what pizza is, you dumb fuck," Taína said. "Of course I like pizza, you dummy, you stupid idiot. Pizza tastes good. Who doesn't like pizza?" she said in perfect English. I was taken aback. She could speak both, probably read in both, too. Taína then laughed like this was the most fun she had ever had.

Doña Flores went to the kitchen, and we were left all alone in the living room. I finally looked up at Taína's face, but my eyes were caught by her breasts. My clothes started to feel really tight, and my eyes would not go above her chin. They simply continued to be stuck there. Taína exhaled like she was bored. Her breasts rose up and then came back down. Her entire gown waved in the air. "Boys, please . . ." She exhaled again and went to her room. She came back wearing a T-shirt over her gown that read: PROPERTY OF THE NEW YORK YANKEES.

"Are you eating well?" I embarrassingly asked in English, as I now knew that Sal had not told me the truth.

"I like Twinkies. You better have brought some. You brought ice cream? Right? Right? And gum, too, stupid? I'll kill you if didn't."

"Yes, yes, yes, I brought gum," I said, but was mad at

myself for not bringing Twinkies. I didn't tell her that Twinkies were bad for you.

"I miss reading magazines," she said, like she was bored. "I like to read. The books in this house are all religious shit, *Watchtower* and *Awake!* shit, really stupid shit."

"Do you want me to get you books?"

"Didn't I just say that? God, you can be so dumb."

"What do you like?"

"Anything, but especially magazines. I like books, but I like magazines more." I remembered the night I followed all three of them as they entered a store.

I wanted to ask her if I should buy her a boom box or an iPod so she could listen to music. I knew she sang. But I didn't know how to get to this point.

"Do you miss school, Taína?" She took a little longer to answer because I think she didn't want her mother to hear us. All she did was shake her head slightly.

"Sometimes. Yeah, I miss school." She shrugged. "I don't miss some of those stupid kids making fun of me."

"Do you miss singing?"

"How'd you know?"

"Ms. Cahill told me—"

"Oh, her? She was nice. Yeah, I sang, no biggie. Just stupid shit."

"Do you want me to get you an iPod?"

"Those things? Why?"

"So you can listen to music," I said, as if it were obvious.

She shrugged like she didn't care, but I knew she did. I didn't know if I should ask her, it was a stupid thing to ask, but I did.

"Can you sing? I mean, just a little. Nothing big."

Taína's mouth quickly opened in disbelief. As if I had asked her for something obscene. As if I had asked her to flash me. She then closed her lips, crossed her arms, and smirked.

"Do you see a hat anywhere?"

"A hat?"

"Yeah, so you can throw in a dollar—I'm not fucking singing for you, bitch."

Doña Flores was done putting away the groceries. She then sat at the kitchen table budgeting the money and making notes on a pad.

I let the singing go and looked straight at Taína's face. I noticed constellations forming around her eyes and nose and I stupidly said out loud, "Taína, you have freckles."

"Fuck you," she snapped. "Yes, I have fucking freckles, and Usmaíl will have freckles, too. You got a problem with freckles?"

"No. I, I like freckles. They're cool."

And then though her belly was big, she had no trouble sitting down on the couch. I sat at the very far end of the couch to give her pregnant body room. Taína scooted over to be closer.

"I hate my name," she said. "Usmaíl is the only name that's not stupid. I like looking out the window at the mailbox. I like to read it in English."

"It's a magical name," I agreed.

"Not like my name. I hate my name. My name is stupid," she said.

"I like your name. It's very pretty." I wanted to kiss her,

but I didn't know how to kiss. I don't think she knew how to kiss either, no matter how much she cursed. But I would never dare. "You know I believe you, Taína." I looked straight at her, tried hard to keep my gaze at her eyes. "I know what has happened to you. I know." I was anxious in telling her. "Something happened inside your body where you got pregnant all by yourself."

"Okay, tell me." She crossed her arms like she was bored.

"Do you know what a cell is?"

"Yes, of course I know what a fucking cell is."

"Okay. Do you know what an atom is?"

"Yes, yes," she said, like she was bored, "everything is made out of them. What is your stupid point?"

"Okay, okay." And I told her about the revolution that had occurred in her body and how she was special and had been chosen by this revolution. How this revolution could not have happened inside any other body. I told her about an atom that refused to follow the law of her DNA. And it rallied other atoms in sharing electrons and expelling them, too, in order to form the molecules needed.

"That is the biggest . . . load . . . of bullshit . . . I have ever heard."

"Fine." I felt her laughing eyes. "Fine. Fine. Then how'd you get pregnant?"

"I don't fucking know, Julio. If I knew, I would tell everybody. I feel really, really stupid, that as a girl I don't know how this happened. But I don't know . . . I don't fucking know."

"You not lying, right?"

"No, I'm not. I really don't know. If I knew I would have told Mami. But I swear I don't know."

I was disappointed she didn't believe me, but I was happy when she scooted her body even closer. For the first time her voice was warm, as if telling me that this was no lie. "I don't remember anything," she said, shaking her head. "I only remember feeling shitty one day and then my mother went to the store and got a stupid fucking test. I peed on it and it said I was freaking pregnant. Worst is I don't remember anything, anything of how it happened, Julio."

"Nothing?" I looked at her bare legs full of gooseberry fuzz and shine.

"I do remember your gifts by the door. We emptied them and threw the boxes away." So my gifts had been accepted after all. What I'd seen on top of the garbage heaps were the hollow boxes.

"But what about the bassinet?" I said, leaving her legs and looking straight at her. "I got you a bassinet and you never took it."

"A bassinet? Come on, shithead"—and she sucked her teeth—"who really needs a bassinet? A crib, yeah, but a bassinet, come on. A bassinet? Who the fuck you think we are, the royal fucking family?" She must have noticed my disappointment or something because her tone became softer.

"I remember you from school. You were nice. You never said mean things to me. I would see you and not be afraid. I would see you from my window standing by the mailbox and feel bad for you." When she saw that my face changed, she changed. "You happy now, God?"

"Fine," I said, as this was whom I had fallen in love with and I did not care. "But you don't feel a revolution inside you? Not even a little bit?"

"Nope. I think that what you told me is pretty stupid. Mami says that only Peta Ponce can get to the truth of what happened."

"The *espiritista*?"

"Yes," Taína said. "And you are paying to bring her."

And I don't know when Taína's hand found my hand and guided it over her warm stomach.

"Usmaíl," she said. And I felt two poles holding up a circus tent. I wanted to giggle, not laugh but giggle, because it was like Usmaíl was inviting me to play. Then the poles went back inside her, but Taína let me keep my hand on her stomach. Taína fixed herself even closer to me and laid her head on my shoulder. She wasn't smiling or anything, but at least she wasn't cursing. I think she was a little tired. Her hair was spilling on my shoulder and I looked at a single strand.

And I saw things.

I saw Taína's DNA.

Its strands wrapped together like hands holding each other, its fingers entwined like ropes. I could see all the subatomic particles, its circuits of atoms like thrilling stars shimmering, pulsating in Taína's inner heavens. I could see deep into the revolution that had given birth to Usmaíl. I saw all this empty, empty space that was not filled up by any form of matter. And then I saw a baby. A baby jumping from atom to atom. There was electricity all around the baby exploding with laughter. And then the baby saw that I was there. I was laughing, too. The baby opened its hands and showed me colors. New colors concealed deep inside stars, new colors existing in hidden dimensions where the chemistry of light is poles apart from the chemistry of our world. Usmaíl showed me prime colors no human had ever seen. All these unseen reds, all the unseen yellows, all the unseen blues, the mystifying colors concealed within the wastes of subatomic supernovas. And then I was back in Spanish Harlem.

Back in the projects.

Back on the couch.

Back to where Taína had fallen asleep on my shoulder. Her pink lips sweetly parted and her breath hinted of orange Cheetos. I was happy that I would take with me the scent of her breath on my shirt. The way her voice seeped into your clothes and you could never wash it out. Taína breathed peacefully. I gently brushed her hair, knowing I would always be in love no matter what insult she dished out. I wanted to be next to Taína, to smell the peach shampoo in her hair, at least that was what it smelled like, to see the tiny hairs inside her ears, to count the freckles on her face. I did not care that Taína did not believe me. I knew a revolution had occurred in her body. I thought about this *espiritista* and thought maybe this Peta Ponce would finally validate the revolution.

Doña Flores entered the living room and found us sitting close to each other but didn't say anything. She just gently tapped my leg. I needed to go. *"Gracias, mijo,"* she whispered so as not to wake her daughter. "*Mira,* Juan Bobo, Ta-te needs her rest."

Verse 4

I WALKED IN with a new dog. My mother was on the phone and the radio was on low volume. I didn't know the singer, though I think it was Juan Luis Guerra, a *bachata*. There was a bag of groceries standing on the couch by the living room. Mom was happy to see the dog because the last time I had given her fifty dollars. My father was very proud of me, too, telling all his pinko friends from Ecuador that I was a man who contributed to the house funds. I wanted to openly contribute more money, but I could not explain all this income I was scamming. So instead, I'd sneak a hundred here and there inside my mom's boot in the closet and she'd never know the difference.

I sat at the table and ate what my father had cooked. Mom kept talking to whoever it was she was on the phone with.

The past day with Taína was all I had been thinking about. I felt like I had been given a gift at seeing some celestial creature that had to be kept secret.

After eating, I fed the new dog that BD and I had borrowed and then gave it water.

I was about to go to Salvador's house when my mother stopped talking on the phone for a second and asked me where was I going.

"To hang with BD."

"You sure?" she said, and excused herself to the person on the other line and got back to me. "Because I got word you were on the second floor knocking at that crazy woman's door."

"Ma, I go to school," I said, insulted, "and now I have a job. I don't have time to do anything."

"*Mira,* Julio, Inelda was seen out on the street buying stuff."

"So?" I shrugged.

"That woman hasn't shown her face and now all of a sudden . . . ?"

"And now what?"

"You still hearing voices?"

"I never heard voices, Ma." But her eyes continued to check my face for things that only mothers can detect.

Then just like that, her face changed and she let it drop. *"Dios te cuide,"* she said. "Don't be home late."

I was about to leave, but this time my father came over from the bedroom.

"Can I walk the dog?" he asked me in Spanish.

What if my dad took the dog for a walk close to the Upper East Side? What if someone recognized the dog? What if then they went to the cops?

"Sure, yeah, okay, Pops, but don't go very far." I chanced

it because it made my father so happy to feel like he was working.

"Thank you. Now, I am not taking away your job," my father said in Spanish. "No one is saying I want to take your job. I just want something to do. That is all." My father went on to put on his best shoes and good clothes because the neighbors would finally see him doing something. My father was even whistling some Ecuadorian song. And this made me happy because I felt like I had hired my dad.

SALVADOR OPENED THE door, covering his eyes from the glaring sun. He was holding a grilled cob of corn with mayonnaise spread all over it and drenched with Tabasco sauce.

"*Mejicanos* eat it like this," he said. "It's not bad. You should try it, *papo*. Me? I'm happy I still have teeth and can eat this, you know, *papo*?"

There were a lot of Mexicans living in Spanish Harlem. Their tastes and food carts were all over the neighborhood. They flew their flag like we flew ours. But now the eagle of their green, white, and red was overtaking the neighborhood. The Mexican flag fluttered all over El Barrio, and it seemed that we liked them and they liked us because there wasn't as much pushing around, as had been the case when we arrived and the Italians wanted to kill us.

"You should try their grilled mangoes," Sal said, letting me in. "That's good stuff. They put *pique* on everything. Man, if I had money I'd eat this every day. It's good, this is a treat for me, you know, *papo*? I'm lucky I don't have high blood pressure, just type two. But who cares, *papo*."

I walked past all the old television sets stacked against the short hallway.

"What are you doing with all these sets, Sal?"

"Gonna fix them, sell them," he said, as if it were obvious.

He must have found them on the sidewalks as he strolled at night. I didn't have the heart to tell him that nobody really bought these old square sets anymore.

"Are you going to fix that piano? Sell it, too," I said, pointing to the biggest thing in the living room.

"No, no," he said. "That was a gift. Hey, you wanna hear something? I can play something for you, *papo*. Really."

"No, it's okay. Here," I said, taking out a wad of twenties.

"You sure?" He could not believe it. "How much you got?"

I told him.

"Okay. That's not so bad." Meaning when he ran this scheme he must have done better. "You need to go after pure breeds. I once borrowed a baby Labrador and man, I struck it rich." He finished his corn and started sucking on the cob. "So, you saw Taína?"

"Yes, she's beautiful, but why does she have to be so nasty sometimes?"

"Really? I never noticed." He picked his teeth a bit.

"She curses all the time, and everything is stupid this, fuck that."

"Never noticed." He licked some mayonnaise off his fingers.

"And you said she can't speak English."

"No, *papo*. I said that she reads the mailbox in Spanish."

"Never mind." I let it go because it was hopeless.

"You want to keep seeing Taína?"

"Of course."

"Then get the money so Peta Ponce can come over here, *papo*," he said, as if there were nothing wrong with this exchange. He opened his refrigerator. "You want something to eat? I got beans. I got cheese. I got bread, and this time they gave us bacon. Don't know where Uncle Sam got the pigs, but it's good bacon, too, *papo*." He saw my look of discomfort. "Listen, *papo*," Salvador said, closing his refrigerator. "I don't blame my sister for what she is doing. You know she grew up during a lot of violence in New York City, you know what I mean, *papo*?"

"So what? My mother did, too. And she's fine."

"That's right, because your mother still has the church. In the church she found her salvation, *papo*. Inelda did, too. But what happens when the church kicks you out, huh? What happens when your line of survival is cut? When Inelda joined the church, she was already a wreck, having grown up with violence, and when she was cut by her church she became desperate. She could pray to God all she wants, but nothing is going to happen. I knew this. I knew this, so I said to her, 'God will send someone to help you.' "

"Who's that?" I said.

"You!" He pointed at my chest. "You, *papo*. God sent you."

"God did not send me." It was the most ridiculous thing I had ever heard.

"I told her He did. You all she has," he said. I knew Doña Flores thought Salvador was a saint, so she'd believe anything her brother told her.

"She can always come back to the church," I said. "They can help her."

"No, she cannot," he said. I saw the *vejigante* costume hanging by the closet was a bit wrinkled and wondered if he had worn it someplace. The *¡Puerto Rico Libre!* button was a bit crooked, too. "Inelda is too far gone. When this happened to Taína and they were kicked out of the church, she lost it completely. She's too far gone, *papo.* Don't you understand that?" And he circled a finger around his ear and whistled. "She's gone. She's cuckoo. You must have seen her talk to walls? And I can't help her because I'm an old man and I'm gone, too, you know, in my own way I'm gone, too, *papo.* Prison—" And he caught himself fast because he had never said the word before. It had slipped out and he tried to lasso the word back into his mouth, but it had already been set free. "It does things to you. You know, for years living with people who are broken beyond repair but continue to live, it does things to you. So when you do leave there, you take that place with you. . . . I'm gone in my own way. Listen, *papo,* poverty is violence. They keep us poor so we can lose it and then they can blame us."

"I don't know. The Man this, the Man that? Come on, Sal," I said, because this all sounded like some excuse.

"Good," he said, noticing me looking at his costume, but he was not going to put it on. "Good. Because if you believe that, *papo,* you stop. You stop right now. You don't borrow any more dogs, and just go home to your mother and her God and never see Taína again. You don't help her or anyone, because if you do, you lose time in running on the poverty treadmill they have placed us on. They are evil people. Poverty is violence, *papo*. And it's worse on women and children."

For the first time I saw anger in el Vejigante's eyes. Anger toward many things, including me. But he would not let that anger be set free, as if he had learned what it had made him do that night long ago.

"Listen, *papo,* they want to keep us poor."

"Who is 'they,' Sal? The Man? Who is the Man? Who is keeping us poor?"

"The capitalist system, the wealthy, the politicians, the police, everyone who benefits from you dying paying rent, *papo*. That's the Man," he said, sounding like someone from another time, another moment, in American history. I knew that I loved Taína, but Sal was becoming this bore. "Violence doesn't always come with a gun, *papo*. It can come with policies that are put in order to keep people like us in their place."

"I got to go." I had come for answers and he had given me politics. I was thinking of not visiting him again. I was going to deal with Doña Flores on my own. Somehow one day soon, I was going to stop borrowing dogs. Help Taína and the baby some other way.

"Later, Sal."

"Hey, *papo* . . ." He stopped me. "I'm gonna tell you this because it belongs to you, okay? It's yours by law. Because, *papo,* when you love someone you burn the sky if you have to in order to feed them."

"I gotta go, Sal."

"Promise me two minutes, okay? I'm an old man, two minutes to me is a lot. But for you, it's a cigarette, okay, *papo*? Just two minutes."

"Fine." I exhaled out of boredom.

"Okay, listen, I was in there for many, many years, but while I was in that place"—and he licked his lips and took a breath—"Inelda was young and she was her family's only source of income. You know how fathers are, never around or never working, so she was it. She liked to sing. She was really good at it, too. You would never know it from looking at her today. But Inelda was great. For years she would kick money my way and my commissary was okay, at least better than most. You know, *papo*." He saw me move toward the door, so he quickened his speech. "She was very popular, had a lot of boyfriends. Then she met this Puerto Rican guy who hated other Latinos. She never married him, but she did live with him. But when Inelda became pregnant, he took off. It was your mother who knew about this doctor who could make sure Inelda never got pregnant again. Inelda didn't want to do this, but the doctor said it was best and she had to feed her mom and soon the baby, too, and after this she could date all the men she wanted with no problems, that doctor said. Your mother agreed with that doctor. You know what I mean, *papo*?" I started to understand why Doña Flores talked to walls. "That was the beginning of my sister's mental problems. All she'd do was cry all day and all night, you know, *papo*, never sang again. Your mother, Julio, was her best friend. And it was your mother who had heard about this woman who was famous around

Puerto Rico and here, too. They say she could heal broken women. Your mother took Inelda to see Peta Ponce."

My mother didn't want me to see Taína. Now I knew why. I felt very sad, like the bottom of my life just fell.

"And Peta Ponce helped Inelda, but she was never the same. Your mother, *papo,* knew about these things because she had been in Inelda's shoes." He cleared his throat and checked my face. "After you were born, *ella lo hizo.* You know, she needed to work to keep you alive, so *ella lo hizo.* It was that or welfare. So when the same thing happened to her friend, your mother did what she only knew, *la operación,* you know. *Ella se lo hizo,* it was so ingrained in the culture that it seemed like nothing. But of course that is not true, otherwise these women wouldn't keep it a secret, and Peta Ponce helped your mother deal with that shit, too."

I had never asked why I had no siblings, but now I knew.

"*Papo,* don't cry. Listen, I got cornflakes, *papo.* I got a banana that's still good. I got these cans of milk, okay, *papo*? Don't cry." But I kept crying. "I can make you a cereal bowl with bananas and powder milk." I kept crying. "Oh, and they gave us soda, don't cry. Listen, you want some soda? Don't know where Uncle Sam found the soda but they gave us soda. You want some soda, *papo*? Don't cry. This *viejo* likes your company, don't cry, man."

Verse 5

AS SOON AS Mom walked in tired from work, I had a bucket of hot water with Epsom salts and the radio turned on. She laughed and called it a miracle. The miracle, I thought, was that she actually let me wash her feet. I sat her on the sofa and removed her shoes. Soledad Bravo sadly, sweetly, and beautifully sang a cover version of "El Violín de Becho."

"Who died?" was all she kept saying as I scrubbed her calves and let her feet soak in hot water. I simply laughed because I had never done this but was happy to be doing it. I had a towel to dry them, too.

"Feeling better, Ma?"

"You want something, right, Julio?" she said.

"No."

Soledad Bravo sang beautifully about a violin that is left alone on a corner.

In the kitchen my father was cooking up a magical storm. Whirlwinds were swallowing up chickens and meats as Ecuadorian spices sprinkled from his fingertips like static electric bolts. He'd throw meats into saucepans that sizzled like an audience clapping and smoke would rise and drift all around the apartment like a blue-gray genie. Our white whale of a refrigerator would open and shut as he mugged it, and then he walked into the living room, angry hands on hips.

"Out of vegetables!" he complained in Spanish. "How can we be out of vegetables?"

The reward flyer had said that the dog was a vegetarian, so I had fed that little yellow dog all the vegetables. I had already taken the vegetarian dog back and collected the hefty reward, but I had forgotten to replace the vegetables.

"I'll go and get some, Pops," I said.

"After you are done," my mother said before going back to humming.

And then, as I continued to wash my mother's feet and as she sang along to such a sad tango, I had a vision.

I saw Mom.

I saw her as a seven-year-old.

A little girl swimming in the Caribbean Sea. She was paddling and smiling and never feeling lonely. The salt water reached her lips as she tasted the Puerto Rican sun. The sky sheltered her from above, and I knew that a child who bathed in those waters could never feel poor. Then I saw her on a plane, then arriving in Spanish Harlem. I saw how she was made fun of by the older kids who had arrived here first. And I saw a little girl in school feeling lost among a sea of children who spoke a language she had yet to understand. I heard her learning those early songs: *"pollito, chicken / gallina, hen / lápiz, pencil / pluma, pen."* In Spanish Harlem my mother felt poor, and the city made sure she felt lonely. I saw her as a sad tropical kid growing up in a freezing tenement. A kid walking home alone after school. The apartment key dangling by a string tied to her lovely neck. Walking among piles and piles of uncollected garbage at her sides. The streets of Spanish Harlem of her time always dirty and broken. A kid coming home to a dark house. How she'd whistle to keep herself company as she did her homework and reheated last night's dinner, waiting for her parents to arrive from their factories. That little girl that would become my mother lived there until the tenement soon met its end by arson, and later she lived in a welfare hotel until the city placed her and her parents in the projects.

And then I saw my mother older but young still.

She was pregnant.

I was still cooking inside her.

I saw her panic. I felt her fear of more children and my father's chronic unemployment. And then I saw her on the hospital table.

And then I was back in our living room.

Back washing my mother's feet.

Back to Soledad Bravo singing.

Ya no puede tocar en la orquesta / Porque amar y cantar eso cuesta.

All that mattered was that Mom was happy. She splashed some water on me while I was getting the towel ready. At that second I felt like a little kid.

My father was grumpy.

"Hurry up." My father huffed. "My food cannot wait." And then he began washing the dishes, caressing them like wet babies in his hands and laying them gently on the drying rack.

I dried my mother's feet and kissed the left one. She pulled it back.

"Gross," she said, but laughed.

"Ma," I said, as I was about to get my father's stuff, "it's going to be all right. Don't worry, it's all going to be all right, okay? It's all going to be fine."

Verse 6

IT'S HARD TO see my mother young and great looking, but she was. Family stories have it that when Mom turned eighteen she convinced her best friend, Inelda Flores, to dye their hair. Mom would be the Blonde and Inelda the Red. She hoped that they'd be known throughout Spanish Harlem as *la Rubia y la Roja,* but everyone simply called them *las Chicas.*

The Girls danced like they were born inside a conga. Mom and Inelda hit all the dance clubs of their day, Corso, the Latin Palace, Palladium, the Tunnel, Boca Chica, Limelight, Cafe con Leche, Tropicana, the Latin Quarter, whether salsa, *charanga,* mambo, merengue, *boogaloo, cumbia, guaracha, plena, bomba,* disco, *bachata,* house, rap, reggae, whatever was playing you could find the Girls, dressed to the tens. They'd eat, drink, and dance. Did they smoke? Of course. Every Saturday on a hot summer night they'd break their religion's rules about not just smoking but socializing with people from the "world." Did they kiss boys? Of course, but that's as far as they went, because what they really lived for was their weekend away from their jobs and families. Mom was a perfume salesgirl, standing all day, spraying people at Gimbels on 86th and Lexington, while Inelda xeroxed other people's documents at Copy Cat across town on the Upper West Side. Both had just graduated from Julia Richman High School on 67th and Second and were enjoying their newfound freedom and small paychecks. I heard my grandparents hated that Mom and Inelda acted this way. "This is what machos do, not ladies," they'd say to them. The Girls lived two lives, one as saints for the elders at their Kingdom Hall of Jehovah's Witnesses and the other as the Girls on an endless quest for the perfect night, the perfect dance number, the perfect drink, the perfect kiss, while breaking hearts that fell and splintered like dropped porcelain. They lived for a sea of scratched records on dance floors built on springs. The Girls liked double-dating boys from the neighborhood who they knew liked to play big shot and spend all their money on them. These clubs were cheap to enter, the price was the long line one had to wait in, but inside it was the drinks that would rob you, hence the big shot boys.

Everything was different then. Many of the Fania All-Stars were old but still kicking and playing. The Girls caught a set at the Palladium with the Joe Cuba Sextet, a nontraditional Latin dance band of old-school architects who had merged black America's R&B styles with Afro-Cuban instruments. The Girls loved how Joe Cuba infused elegance by adding cool violins and smooth flutes to his band's sound in order to balance the macho horn section. The Girls loved Joe Cuba because his *boogaloo* was so conducive to spinning, and what girl does not like to be spun?

On payday, they'd hit Casa Latina on 116th Street and spend a good chunk of what was left of their hard-earned money on records and cassettes; they'd hit Casa Amadeo in the Bronx, too. Later, the Girls would grab a ghetto blaster and walk to the north side of Central Park to sunbathe. They'd turn the dial in search of old dance tunes, Machito's "Live from the Copacabana, 1959" or "Celia Cruz en El Club Flamingo Havana, 1965," broadcast on WHNR or WMEG. They'd bring their own drinks and ice and let the sun bake them like *gandules*. Back then, kids fished the Harlem Meer, teens on Rollerblades skated by, and families barbecued. A different city, crime was high, and they lived with it. The Girls knew to stay together and that all it took was common sense, a little luck, and safety would take care of itself. Just stay together was their mantra, never to be broken. Stay together. They knew the places to go in Central Park and which places not to. It was the same on Saturday nights: they knew to always have cab money—don't take the subway after nine p.m. But the dance clubs, that was where the gloves came off. The Girls would do as the music dictated but always staying together.

I've seen pictures of my mother back then, thin, push-up bra, fake blond hair, fake green eyes, legs for days, and a waist so thin it looked like she could be cut in half. Mom looked too beautiful to be real because, simply, she wasn't. Her Taíno cheekbones, olive skin, red puffy lips, and Indian features contrasted so heavily with the long, lush, dyed blond hair and green contacts that no matter how striking, how gorgeous, you knew it had to be fake. God or nature could never dish out that much color to any single person. But the men never cared. Family legend has it that one night at the Park Palace on 110th Street and Fifth, as the Girls were fanning their sweaty faces after a Wilfrido Vargas merengue—*Mami, el negro está rabioso / Quiere bailar conmigo*—a man dressed like it was still 1970 with the widest shirt collar and elephant bell-bottoms asked my mother if she wanted to be on the cover of his next LP. The Girls recognized Héctor Lavoe immediately. In front of them was one of the people who had invented their reason to live. Speechless and hot and flattered, they did what most girls do when together: they went to the restroom and had a conference. Like everyone who loved the Fania All-Stars, the Girls knew that Lavoe was not really a skirt chaser. All he cared about was his music and what he shot up his arm. So they figured it was safe and Inelda would tag along just in case, remembering their mantra, "Stay together." This would be their secret. If the church elders ever found out, my mother would deny it, she'd tell her elders that it wasn't her, looked like her, but it wasn't her and Inelda would back her. They had a plan.

The shoot was to be at Orchestra Records in Harlem, 1210 Lenox Avenue, at one p.m. That's all the information Lavoe had given the Girls, nothing about what to wear, what to bring, what to sign. Nothing. When they arrived and checked their names at the security desk, the recording studio was empty. They waited. The first person to show up was the lighting guy. A long-haired kid from Long Island with two first names: Frank Christopher. All Frank did was talk about opening a jazz club on 103rd and Broadway. He set the lights and took tons of Polaroid pictures of Mom from all angles and sides of her face. "Jazz is missing on the West Side these days." And he'd take a picture. "I'm going to call it Smoke. You girls should drop by, give you free drinks." But jazz was not in the hearts of these girls, they loved the heat of salsa, and now one of them was going to be on an album cover belonging to one of their gods. They waited. Then the photographer arrived. A middle-aged woman with white hair, yellow teeth, and butchy-looking shoes and jeans. She took from Frank the Polaroids of Mom and studied them, looking for Mom's best angles. She asked the Girls if they wanted anything. It was now six p.m. and they were hungry and she told them to go out and eat, nothing was going to happen until Héctor got here. And then she said in Spanish, *"Héctor se está pullando, y viene cuando le dé la gana."* They were taken aback because they had never heard a white woman talk in such clear, precise Spanish, and she had told them what they as seasoned *salseras* already knew: Lavoe was getting high. His band knew it; that's why they were not there. Everyone knew it. Nothing was going to happen until at least midnight. That's why the studio was empty. My mother asked what she was going to be wearing, what she was going to be doing in the picture. The photographer laid out the shoot. Told Mom that she would be lying in her underwear on an ironing board as Héctor Lavoe and Willie Colón's band surrounded her, mimicking ironing movements and holding hot irons in their hands. Oh, and that depending on what underwear she had on, if

Lavoe liked it, she could be in the picture wearing it, otherwise she would have to be nude on the ironing board. The album title was *La Plancha.*

They continued to have fun and be the Girls and never crossed lines that would hurt them or their families religiously. Soon, eighteen became twenty-eight, and for motherless, single Latinas this was the kiss of death. Both their respected parents kept bugging them, expecting the Girls to get married and have kids, keep a home, *"se van a quedar jamonas,"* they'd say to them, *"con sólo gatos."* But they continued to work hard and dance even harder. Soon, my mother passed a civic test and was now a city clerk for the MTA, and Inelda was now a receptionist for a chic facial surgery doctor in midtown, and they continued to party. Most of their checks belonged to their families, but the weekends were for *las Chicas.*

My mother's crazy recording studio photo shoot experience never left Inelda. Or better said, she never forgot the recording studio. Inelda always sang. Back at Julia Richman High School she sang in plays, assemblies, and fashion shows. You could hear Inelda's soulful Latin voice at block parties, weddings, bridal showers, parades. Never in church, though, as Jehovah's Witnesses don't really get down the way Pentecostals do on street corners, which would have made Inelda a star at her church. Karaoke was just getting introduced in America, but it had not reached New York City, let alone Spanish Harlem. Inelda wanted to sing. She loved Lisa Lisa, Prince, Stacy Lattisaw, worshipped Irene Cara, Alison Moyet solo or with YAZ, Teena Marie, especially "Lovergirl," the Latin Rascals, Brenda K. Starr, Olga

Tañon, the Cover Girls, Expose, Luther Vandross, and for a while she couldn't get enough of Jon Secada; but her soul belonged to anything or anyone related to salsa. Inelda had seen flyers at Orchestra Records advertising auditions for backup singers. It seemed they were always calling for backup singers. And so the Girls returned ten years later, only this time it was so Inelda could sing.

The Girls arrived together, always together, along with other hopeful singers, and cleared security and then went up the narrow stairs that led to the recording studios of Orchestra Records, where everything was produced on the cheap. They made a lot of 78s that broke as easily as eggshells, by mostly unknown singers and bands that Orchestra Records hoped would take off. But many would sell only a few hundred copies, and the rest would end up in milk crates on the floors of botanicas such as San Lázaro y Las Siete Vueltas, Otto Chicas, and El Congo Real or in barbershops of Latino neighborhoods in American cities. Outside of a red door marked STUDIO was a small waiting room where the Girls sat on folding chairs and lingered along with others to be called. On the wall were taped pictures of the labels' stars. There was a glass window into the studio, and the Girls could see the musicians setting up their brass instruments, their liquor bottles on the floor next to them. The studio was about the size of a big kitchen, with corked walls to keep the sound in and two large RCA microphones in the center and another four mics for the studio musicians. The horn players would sit on one side of the room, and the rhythm section of drummers, conga players, timbales, bass, and piano would be on the other side of the room, some standing, as it was crowded and many had to improvise their spaces. The center was reserved for the singer. Inelda's name was called. It was her time to shine. But family lore has it that what happened in this fairy tale was that when Inelda was about to audition, a frog showed up disguised as a prince and swept Mom away.

I know what happened next only because as a little kid I loved it when my parents invited friends over for drinks. They'd play old music, drink too much, and talk about things that should have stayed caged. They'd tell me to go to bed, but I would stay up in my room, my ear glued to the door, and listen to the adults talk. I'd hear my half-drunk parents tell stories about their youth. It was during one of these small parties, when I was about twelve, that I heard about Bobby *"el Pollo con la Voz"* Arroyo. He was a *salsero* whom Orchestra Records was betting high on. They had spent a good amount of money on him and his Mercedes-Benz was proof. He had the swagger of a Latin lover's walk as if he were the last Coca-Cola in the desert. I heard that Bobby had a good voice, not great but good. He was, though, a great lyricist and could compose on the fly, the second coming of Lavoe, who had just died. His arrangements needed help, though, and he wasn't that great of a songwriter either. Orchestra Records was going to surround him with the best talent they had, as the cosmos was trembling for his debut. His looks were devastating. But what made him so marketable wasn't so much his good looks but rather that Bobby could boast being the American-born son of four Latino nationalities, and not just four, the Big Four. His mother was Puerto Rican and Cuban. His father was Dominican and Mexican. Orchestra Records heard cashiers ringing all over the Americas and especially in U.S. cities such as New York, Chicago, Miami, Boston, D.C., and LA. Puerto Ricans, Dominicans, Chicanos, and Cubans could all claim Bobby *"el Pollo con la Voz"* Arroyo as theirs.

In my family, like most families, they led us kids to believe that our mother had only ever been in love with our father and vice versa. Not true. I know about Bobby only because of the gossip that gets spread around at parties by friends, neighbors, and at church, or as I just recently was told by Salvador of other things of which I was clueless. It's these secrets that birth more secrets when a family tries to cover them. I heard my mother fell madly in love with Bobby. They were always together, whether on the beach or at La Marqueta, she'd always place her arm around him as if she had known him all her life. In summer they'd go to Coney Island. In winter ice skating at Lasker Rink or bowling—yes, bowling—at the 42nd Street Port Authority. But the nights were for his salsa gigs, which if in New York City my mother never failed to attend, and then the party afterward, which my mother, who still lived with her parents, could not attend. Each time he would say to Mom, "*Sólo un chin, un chin, mami,* just a few minutes." But this meant he'd stay all night. Mom would have to leave all by herself, but it mattered little to her. My mom was willing to marry this guy—it would be a bad thing to marry a non–Jehovah's Witness, but at least she'd be leaving her father's house by the Book. But this was impossible, because, you see, Bobby *"el Pollo con la Voz"* Arroyo was already married with kids.

But soon, Bobby's career soured as fast as it had been sweet, as there was, and always will be, only one Héctor Lavoe. Bobby's debut sales were laughable. Super KQ or La Mega wouldn't play his single "Apriétame La Cintura"; same for other Spanish stations. His manager bullied Orchestra Records to release what he felt was a more danceable single, "Tirando a Pelota," to the same results. Soon, gigs became hard to book. His manager convinced Orchestra Records to take a gamble and foot the bill for a big free summer concert in Central Park. It rained for three days, and when the sun showed its face, there were more mosquitoes on the grass than people. His manager had Orchestra Records pair him with other established acts on the bill, but he had so little draw that these acts didn't want him. They lost money carrying *"el Pollo con la Voz"* on their bill. They mutinied. Threatened to leave when their contracts were up and go to Fania.

But my mother still loved Bobby. After work she would make the easy trek of taking a crosstown bus from Spanish Harlem to the Upper West Side and to Yogi's, a country-western bar where Bobby drank all day. She would sit with Bobby *"el Pollo con la Voz"* Arroyo in a bar where no sounds that escaped the country music jukebox could drift him back to a failed past. She'd make excuses for him. That he had been under too much pressure. The fault lay with Orchestra Records. The fault lay with his manager. They had chosen the wrong singles to release. They had overlooked the good numbers, the ones that showcased his voice and had a great tin-tirin-tin-tin salsa beat that was irresistible. My mother would blame everyone but Bobby, and I think this made him more like a saint in her eyes. Most nights my mother had to put a drunken Bobby in a cab and take him back to his wife. Leave him at the door, hoping that his wife would find him outside their apartment. She never met his kids, never met his wife, but they both knew about each other. And one night as my mother brought a drunk Bobby home, his wife had left her a note outside the door: "I put up with him because he pays my rent. But you?"

Then one night at Yogi's, as David Allan Coe sang about picking up his mother from prison, the public phone on the wall next to this big wooden bear rang. The barmaid answered it. She didn't know how, but he knew Bobby *"el Pollo con la Voz"* Arroyo drank there. She covered the mouthpiece and yelled toward Bobby, who sat next to my mother, "Your manager!"

I'm sure Bobby and my mom must have felt a surge of hope. A belief in a God that doesn't let you hit rock bottom.

"They want me to make a record?" Bobby said over the phone.

"No, Bobby, that's the last thing they want."

At Orchestra Records was this fresh, great-looking kid, a genius *reggaetón* singer, Puerto Rican Colombian Nicaraguan Honduran, and like his background, his music was a signature of everything. It had licks of salsa, merengue, hip-hop, even Latin jazz, all tied up by his *reggaetón* kicks. His sales were projected to be astronomical, and since his last name was also Arroyo, he wanted to be the one and only *"Pollo."* He bullied Orchestra Records to get that name back. The record company had no choice. They thought of a promo to be shown all over Telemundo, where they would re-create the kitchen where they had shot Bobby *"el Pollo con la Voz"* Arroyo's only and last video, get some dancers dressed the same exact way, and then have Bobby come on-screen to utter, *"Yo ya estoy cocinaó."* And the kid would come on-screen, push Bobby aside, and start singing in a breakneck-speed *reggaetón, "Yo soy el nuevo pollo, el único con orgullo, Jessie Arroyo. Tú tienes un hoyo, cuidado con mi pollo."* It was a hit. Bobby was paid two hundred bucks and then went back to his slow flickering.

Inelda?

The "Stay together" mantra?

My mother had wrapped herself around this guy like a recurring melody and had forgotten all about her best friend. At the Orchestra Records' audition, Mom had left Inelda flat the second Bobby showed up and said, *"Mami, ¿cual es tu nombre?"* I would love to say that I was told in detail how beautifully Doña Flores sang that day, years ago. I would love to say that in my family we have talked about the day when Inelda's voice put Mercedes Sosa to shame. From family friends and church gossip, all I have about that day are bits and pieces on how Inelda sang a bolero a cappella. And how the people in that room were changed. Inelda's voice told everyone that Latinas can sing sad songs like no other people because they are not really singing. They are telling the story of our suffering and how this suffering is a bridge to one another and how all of us must cross this bridge or we will die. I have heard that when Inelda finished her number, you could hear a mouse piss on cotton. But afterward, Inelda never showed up to Orchestra Records again. She was afraid of going alone. Her best friend dumped her, and later, she hid further into herself. I don't know more about Doña Flores than this. All I know is that that must be the voice Taína inherited.

What happened to Mom later is where things get foggy like shower curtains, images become opaque and blurry. It started with a black eye. That Bobby was so drunk, one night *"El mejor sonero del mundo, sí, señor,"* after taking another swig of whiskey, bashed my mother's eye. Told her to shut up. He'd heard enough and that all those excuses she was making for him didn't matter. He was the best. He was still great no matter what anybody said, better than all of them. *"Lavoe,"* he yelled before they were both thrown out of that bar, *"era un canario en heroína. Pero yo, yo soy el pollo con la voz."*

That night, my mother arrived at her parents' disheveled, scared, and crying. I have been told neighbors saw her. Family and friends saw her. Everyone saw her. Everyone heard what had happened or had his or her own version. Some say that it was something worse than a black eye. Why would her parents be so ashamed that they'd take my mother on a "vacation" to Panama? Why would they leave town, like Mary did when she got pregnant? I don't know. When I was twelve and secretly listening to the adults talk from my room, what stands out is not what my mom went through or what happened to Inelda. What stands out is never, ever, hearing my father say a word. All her other friends would cut Mom off, laugh a little, or ask something, but never did I hear my father. I can only picture him silent, staring straight ahead, a beer in hand, letting Mom tell a story he could do nothing about. A story that maybe my mother should have never told. Or at least not in front of him.

YOU KNOW WHO loves you by the gifts they bring you. The gifts don't have to cost a lot, they just need to reflect a part of you and of the other person. There is this colorful bookstore on 103rd between Park and Lexington called La Casa Azul. It has a blue canopy and a sidewall mural featuring both Mexican icons such as Frida Kahlo and Nuyorican poets such as Pedro Pietri, along with a lot of skeletons. I asked the great-looking Chicana lady, Aurora Anaya, who owned the place, if she could suggest books that a girl of fifteen would like. She gave me some titles. I bought them along with a book on the origin of the universe. I then took the 6 downtown. I bought an iPod and magazines for Taína, an alligator shirt for BD, a camera for Sal, linen sheets for Doña Flores's new bed, and cooking utensils for my father. For my mother, flowers, earrings, and a José Luis Perales *Exitos* CD. I was happy with all my purchases because I felt in my gifts they'd see what I saw in them. And in my gifts they could read how much they cared for me.

"ARE YOU SURE these aren't hot?" Mom said when I gave her the earrings.

"Ma," I said, "I bring you a gift and you accuse me of stealing?"

"Está bien, Julio. Pero . . ." She bit her lower lip because

she liked them. "You washed my feet the other day, now you bring me jewelry? Huh? I don't know—"

"My job is going great, Ma." I saw my father in the kitchen excitedly opening the fridge to see what he could cook up with his new utensils.

"Did you read the *Watchtower* magazine I left you?" Mom asked me.

"Yes," I lied to make her happy.

"And you know you have a doctor's appointment," she said, holding her earrings tight. "Do you still believe that Taína got pregnant by herself?"

"Again?" I sighed. "Again?"

"Do you?"

"You do," I said jokingly. "You go to church every Sunday to say hi to her Son." But I could not tease her much. Sometimes I could, but now things were different.

"You know what I mean," she said, a bit annoyed. "You just better go to your doctor's appointment."

"Of course," I said, because after what I knew Mom had gone through she could do no wrong.

"Yo voy contigo."

"Ma, no," I protested, only because going to the doctor with your mother is embarrassing. "I'm seventeen, I can go by myself—"

"Or not go and say you went. So I am going with you, *y se acabó,*" she said, and then headed over to the stereo to play her new José Luis Perales CD.

Quisiera decir / Quisiera decir tu nombre . . .

My father closed the refrigerator.

"I know what to cook," he shouted in Spanish. "I am

going to go out and get the ingredients to make *seco de chivo.*"

Ecuador's version of Puerto Rico's *asopao.*

"I hate that, Silvio." My mother forgot about humming. "I don't eat deer. You better not go out and buy venison."

"You ever tried it? . . . No? So how do you know you will not like it?"

"*Ay bendito,* I don't need to have a hole in my head," Mom said, "to know I don't want a hole in my head."

"I am going to make it anyway," he said. "And *seco de chivo* is just the name. It does not have to have venison, it can be made with chicken."

"I don't care," Mom said. "I'm not serving you."

"Fine," he said, "me and Julio will eat, and I will serve us."

They both looked my way.

I was to choose who was right.

Once my father lost his job, cooking became the only power he had in the house. Mom brought in the money and now I was bringing in money, too. My father wanted to make this Ecuadorian dish because it was his way of saying he had some control in this house. They were both the same people, I thought. My mother loved Puerto Rico, but that was the past, and the closest thing to it was Spanish Harlem. But my father never felt this way about New York City. It was the Ecuador of his communist youth that sustained him.

The day would come, my father liked to lecture in Spanish at the dinner table, when the New Man will be born and bring with him a New Order where all rent collectors and welfare pimps will be hanged by their underwear, he'd say, sounding like Fidel Castro. As a little kid, it was a day I, too, awaited. When would it come? I knew no rent meant more money for us to spend. Maybe more money for us to buy fresh meat and not have to eat leftovers day after day. Maybe money for me to have a second pair of jeans, a second pair of sneakers, and, if anything was left over, maybe a movie. My father's communist pamphlets were full of pictures of happy and strong men working the harvest, their busty wives bringing them water, apples, and bread as little kids like me picked flowers. Above us a smiling Red Comrade Lenin provided in abundance for all.

Es Jehovah, my mother would counter, that will destroy all the wicked people and turn the earth into a paradise. A New Order will come, but by Jehovah. As a little kid, it was a day I, too, awaited. When would it come? My mother's *Watchtower* magazines portrayed that glorious paradise with these colorful pictures of happy and strong men working the harvest, their busty wives bringing them water, apples, and bread and little kids like me playing with baby tigers, baby lions, baby zebras, and eating all the fresh fruit they could munch on. Above us the hand of an invisible Jehovah provided in abundance for all those on earth.

My parents met not here but in Panama. My dad had been kicked out of Ecuador for being a communist. They don't kill you in Ecuador: they give you a one-way ticket to anywhere in Central America. He chose Panama and not Nicaragua because a revolution in Panama was still possible, while Nicaragua was like operating on a healthy person. There he met my mom. She was on vacation with her parents. She was more depressed than a weeping willow. Her parents thought it might do her good to leave the country and take in some sun. Or maybe it was because of the shame that the Bobby singer incident had brought them; they just wanted to forget the whole thing had actually happened. I never really knew. All I know is she saw this commie punk who, family legend has it, saw her and sent her a note: *"Cuando te ví flores crecieron en mi mente."* And that was the beginning. My mother loved bad boys, and she actually thought that my dad was one because he had been thrown not just out of a bar but out of an entire country. She couldn't have been more wrong.

My father, like most Latin American communists, just talks a good revolution. My father considered the United States the enemy. The capitalist who will rip the tusk of the last elephant in Kenya for a two-bedroom in East Hampton, he'd say. They will cut down the last rubber tree in Brazil for a Diners Club card. They have no friends because they have subscribed to the law of dog eat dog and will eat one another should the stock market allow it. My children will be born not under a capitalist green sky but under a blue one, he'd say to her. The thing was that my mom was hot. She still dyed her hair blond and wore the green contact lenses, tight dresses highlighting more curves than an American highway. And she told him about this place in New York City, where everyone spoke Spanish. There was no need to learn English. He could find a job easily, as he had an engineering degree from the University of Guayaquil. That magical place was El Barrio. In Manhattan. So they got married, and by the time my father found out this was not so, that his degree from Ecuador was useless, that he needed to learn English, and that jobs were not that easy to find—I was conceived.

"I'll eat it," I said, to make my father feel good. "I'll eat the *seco de chivo*." He did cook, after all, and I'd try it.

"Disgusting," Mom said. "I'll go out and get some food. Rice, *gandules, pasteles, chuletas, pechuga de pollo,* you know? Normal food."

"And what is normal food?" my father asked.

"What I just told you."

"That is normal for you, but in China—"

"We're not in China," she said. "I want normal food."

My father decided not to argue. He huffed and puffed. He went to put on his shoes. The new lapdog I'd borrowed was lying on a pillow bed next to them. Without saying a word to me, my father took the leash and put it on the dog. I wanted to tell Pops he couldn't take the dog, but my father was mad. He also thought by walking the dog and shopping, he was killing two birds with one stone. So I let him. I went to my room and picked out clean clothes. When I was all dressed, I picked up Taína's iPod, books, and magazines. On my way out the door, I saw my mother looking at herself in the bathroom mirror. The earrings dangled from both sides of her smiling face and she was humming. *Quisiera decir / Quisiera decir tu nombre.*

Verse 7

WITH AN IPOD, a gallon of ice cream, groceries, Blow Pops, Starburst, bedsheets, books, magazines, and biodegradable diapers, because I had read plastic diapers hurt the environment, and with an envelope full of money, I knocked. I no longer had to wait.

"Come in, *papo*. Come in." It was Sal. "This is not my house so I can't offer you food, you know?"

"It's okay," I said. "I already ate."

"Us, too. I mean if I knew you were coming . . . Next time, next time, okay, *papo*?" And he helped me stack up the diaper boxes against the wall and took the groceries to the kitchen.

There was a brand-new flat-screen television hanging on the living room wall. It was tuned to Telemundo. A variety program where there was a scantily dressed woman bending over to fill a cup of water from the office water cooler. A man was trying to make copies nearby, and when his eyes caught the woman's ass, the Xerox machine started ejecting paper everywhere. The laugh track volume was really low, as if Doña Flores didn't want any of the neighbors to hear that she, like many Latinos, liked this kind of humor. It's old humor. Slapstick with very little intelligence, but that's what our parents liked to watch. I saw that the couch was draped in blankets and pillows. At first, I thought it must be where Salvador had slept the night before. But I soon realized that it was really where Doña Flores slept, as this was a one-bedroom and Taína had her own room. I looked for Taína. The door to her room was closed.

Salvador went to get his half-sister. She was in the bathroom and he knocked. When Doña Flores came out, she was glowing as if she were the one that was pregnant. The first thing she asked for was the money. I gave her the envelope. Doña Flores's eyes became moons. She didn't ask how I or my mother was doing. Nothing. All she said was, *"Juan Bobo, Ta-te está en su cuarto. Sólo toca antes de entrar, ¿okay?"* And Doña Flores and Salvador sat together at the kitchen table. They budgeted the money as they talked quietly about Peta Ponce.

I had never seen Taína's bedroom or any girl's bedroom, and I didn't know what to expect. When I gently knocked and said my name, I heard Taína's agitated voice, "*¡Coño!* Now I gotta put on clothes. Wait!" And with ice cream and books and magazines in hand, I nervously waited. "Fine. Come in, dummy," she said from the other side.

I opened the door and walked in. I didn't close the door all the way, leaving a ray of light to guiltily escape from her bedroom and into the living room, where the television stayed on.

Taína's room smelled of baby talcum powder mixed with some sweet, lowly scented peach soap. Her walls were not pink, like I had thought all girls' rooms were, but an off-white, like moths. She had no posters of movie stars or kittens or puppies or anything other than a mirror on the wall. A multicolored rug covered most of the floor, and her dresser was a dark crimson that matched her sheets, comforter, and pillows. The crimson was a good color, I thought, because dark red hid spots and dirt. I always drooled when I slept, and so I had red sheets, too, to hide my drool.

Taína looked at what I was carrying. She went not for the ice cream or the magazines but for the books. She took them off my hands and slowly sat her pregnant body back down on her bed. Her back leaned against the headboard, where she had placed a pillow to hold herself up. She patted the side of the bed next to her, commanding me to sit down. Her bed was a frightful mess of Cheetos crumbs, Doritos, popcorn, and chips. I wondered, Where were the roaches? They must love her as much I did. I nervously sat next to her. I felt our thighs rub against each other on the bed. My circuitry exploded, and yet it felt as natural as breathing.

"You dummy, you stupid idiot, take your shoes off. Don't dirty up my bed." She took the Blow Pops and thought about having one but had a Starburst instead.

The bed was full of crumbs, so I didn't know what she was talking about. But I took my shoes off anyway and placed them neatly on the floor and sat beside her again. Taína had thrown a T-shirt over the same gown she always wore, but this time it had fewer wrinkles, as if it were a new one. The gown covered her legs but not her lovely feet, whose thick ankles were full of water. It would be only a few weeks before Usmaíl's arrival.

"I like your room," I said. Taína shrugged. She continued to read the books' jackets. Her lips barely moved, as if she were silently praying. There was a glow behind her like in paintings of saints at the Met. I don't want to sound dumb, but I saw it. It was a golden glow that hovered around her head as if there were a light behind Taína. But then the glow dimmed and faded.

"These books are fucking great!" She pressed them to her breasts as she crossed and uncrossed her legs that lay on the bed.

"Do you want ice cream?" I said, because it would melt soon if she didn't put it away. "I brought you ice cream. I got ice cream—"

"No, I don't want fucking ice cream. Did you bring me gum?"

I forgot.

I panicked and she knew it. Taína exhaled and shook her head.

"It figures. Can't you do anything right? Next time you better freaking bring some."

So I placed the ice cream on the floor next to my shoes and I gave her the iPod. I told her that I had already connected it to the Internet Wi-Fi we have at home and all she had to do was create her own account and stream all the music she wanted.

"Really?" She was excited but didn't believe me.

"Yes," I said.

Taína knew how to work the iPod. She quickly made an account for herself and smiled as she typed it in.

"Want to know my password?" she said. I nodded. "Okay, it's Bigbichos2000." She was trying hard to hide her excitement and not laugh.

"Good password"—not knowing what else to say—"hard to break that one."

Having music in her house again made her happy. And for two seconds, she hummed. It had a nice melody and it was as close to hearing her sing as I had gotten. I think she wanted to hum some more, but she seemed nervous. She then hid the iPod and earphones under the mattress. "Mami can't see this."

"Why?" I said. "It's only for music, really."

"She says that music disturbs the spirits."

"Oh."

"Yeah, she says that the spirits will be confused and forget what happened to me if they hear music."

"You think that's true?"

"Well, if it is, then those are some really fucking stupid spirits," she said. "But I don't want to get Mami upset. I'll listen when Mami is asleep."

And I let that go.

Taína went back to her books.

I had brought her *Under the Feet of Jesus, Caramelo, When I Was Puerto Rican,* and *How the Garcia Girls Lost Their Accents.* Taína couldn't have been happier, but when she saw the book about the universe, her eyes shot up at me.

"What . . . the . . . fuck . . . is this shit?"

"It's the origin of us," I said. "I mean all of us, everything, planets, the sun, other galaxies, everything. How it all started."

Cosmos was a big coffee-table book with colorful pictures of nebulas and galaxies and told of the birth of the universe. I had looked at it many times in the school library. I liked the pictures. But what I really liked was how it explained everything in easy and common terms. It talked down-to-earth in a language that everybody could easily understand.

"See, Taína"—*Cosmos* made me feel and sound smart—"the universe, like Usmaíl, created itself, too, see?" She began thumbing through the pictures. "It's like what's happened in your body. One atom asked another atom if they could join and that atom said, 'Yes.' Sort of the way the universe began with the word 'yes.' There was nothing, just these particles floating, and then one particle asked another particle to join and that particle said, 'Yes,' and boom, a big bang. It just happened. In the beginning was the word. But the word was 'yes.' See, no need for a Father, or a God. Or anything. Just a yes."

"Yes," Taína said, sneering. "Yes, if you ask me if this book fucking sucks? Yes." She threw the book aside. "And don't bring up that stupid revolution, please. I already threw up today and I'll kill you if you make me vomit again."

But I still told her about the universe becoming sentient out of a dead nothing. What had happened to her was something similar. How long ago all these proteins and amino acids floated in goo, in some womb-like ditch here on earth millions of years ago. We came out of those slimy puddles, just like babies do.

"Where's a picture of those fucking puddles?" she demanded, opening *Cosmos* again. I think this got her attention, as she thumbed through the pictures more carefully. I examined her small hands and saw her grubby fingernails. But the dirt stuck between them did not matter to me at all.

I showed her the picture of a young, volcano-like earth and told her the puddles were there.

"No way." She pouted. "I don't see shit." She closed the book. "I'm getting bored and you didn't bring me gum. And your shoes did dirty my bedcovers, you dummy, you stupid idiot."

"Listen, Taína, a revolution was fought inside your body, okay—"

"Okay nothing. Stop!" She exhaled loudly and her stomach rose like a mountain. "That is why Mami wants that Peta Ponce bitch to come over, okay? The *espiritista* helped her after I was born. I know all about it, okay? What Mami did to herself." I knew what Taína meant. Sal had told me. It was then I realized that things like this are easy to repress. They are so horrible you do your best to forget them, and soon, you fool yourself into thinking that it never happened. "And Mami says the *espiritista* will help me, too. She will get the truth out of me." And tossing *Cosmos* aside like a dirty diaper, she said, "And I know, Julio, that that stupid *espiritista* bitch ain't gonna say shit about some stupid fucking revolution fought inside my body, okay? So fucking drop it."

"How do you know Peta Ponce won't say anything about a revolution in your body?"

"Because I know."

"How do you know?"

"I just know."

"How do you know?"

"Because I just fucking know!"

With not too much trouble Taína got up from the bed and stood in front of the mirror. "What I know is that this thing in my eye is killing me. Come over here," she ordered, and tilted her head back, prying her left hazel eye open to try to get rid of a speck of dust. "Blow on it, gently. . . . Not so hard, you dope," she said.

I nervously held her warm temples gently and stood face-to-face. I was seven inches taller than Taína's five feet one inch and I was looking down at her saintly eyes. "Bastard is there"—her eyes wiggled—"I can feel the fucker. . . ." I gently blew on her rolling hazel eyeball. "Easy, easy, you dummy, you stupid idiot. Easy." Her body tensed up, only to slacken once again. Then her adorable lips parted. I felt the heat of her round stomach against mine. Then my lips touched the dry, rough corners of hers with a tiny quick peck until with an impatient wriggle my lips pressed onto Taína's lips. And the world became new.

I tasted Cheetos in her saliva mixed with lemon Starburst.

Taína pulled back and wiped her lips against my shoulder. Her cheeks were flushed, her lips were still glistening, and she brushed a strand of hair aside. I braced for an insult.

"When Peta Ponce comes," she said nicely, "I want you to be there, okay?"

"Okay."

"Promise."

"Yes."

"No, you better promise."

"Yes, yes, I promise," I said.

"Okay, good."

She held the door open for me.

"That was nice," she said. "That was very nice. Fucking awesome, actually. And thanks for the iPod. I can't wait till Mami is asleep. Bring me Twinkies next time, okay?" And she smiled a tiny smile, shot me an air kiss before closing her bedroom door.

Verse 8

"SHE WAS WALKING aim-less-ly in Central Park," I said, and the dog owner saw little Ralphy wailing. "Our little brother loves her, but when we found out she was lost, we brought her back to you." This time the lady went for the reward right away.

"You get him a dog just like Mrs. Dalloway," she said, though that was my line, and she didn't even wait for little Ralphy to cry on BD's fake arm.

"It's a pure Cavalier King Charles Spaniel." She said a name that sounded expensive, but I simply thought that it looked like the dog in the Disney movie *Lady and the Tramp*. "This should be enough to get one just like her. You've no idea how happy you have made me," she said, kissing her dog, who barked a quick thank-you to me for taking care of her. We exited the doorman building a block away from the Guggenheim Museum. This reward was big, and I had now opened up a bank account. Had gotten the forms, and though my mother had told me not to trust banks, she still cosigned at Banco Popular on 106th Street and Third Avenue. I now deposited all the reward checks there. I gave BD his cut, gave Sal some, Mom some, gave my dad some, hid some inside Mom's boot without telling her, and gave the rest to Doña Flores.

I brought Taína gum and Twinkies.

"These are bad for you," she scolded me. "You want me to get fat? I can't fucking believe you. Don't you give a fuck about me?" she said. I didn't know if she was joking because she was fat, she was pregnant. But she kissed my cheek and I was happy. Doña Flores was asleep in Taína's room, so without asking, I placed my hand on Taína's stomach. Touching her stomach was a sensation that I knew was not going to come back. It was as fleeting as the life of soap bubbles. Once Usmaíl arrived this, too, would be over. So I kept my hand on her stomach, feeling Usmaíl kicking. Taína slapped my hand away. "Okay, stupid, what the fuck, enough, you wanna play patty-cake with the baby? God." But then she took my hand and led me to the couch. The television was on.

"Rub my feet." I didn't know if I heard that right. "Come on, what are you waiting for? Rub . . . my . . . feet."

I was paralyzed with happiness. Taína turned her body toward the edge and lay back against the couch's arm, her moon stomach now facing the ceiling. She placed her feet on top of my lap at the other end of the couch. I took one foot in my hands and it was warm. It hinted of body lotion mixed with mothballs. I wanted to kiss her foot.

"I don't know how to do this," I said shyly. But Taína's eyes were closed as she made a moan of half-pleasure, half-sleep. Taína squirmed a little. The more I massaged her feet, the more she squirmed and the higher her gown would ride up on her. My clothes felt so miserably tight I thought they would break out. I took full advantage in studying her bare legs.

"I want more books, Julio," she said with eyes still closed. I was happy to hear her voice, as I did not know where I was at the moment or what part of Taína I was looking at. "I liked the one about the farmer workers. I liked Estrella. That Viramontes book was good, the others kinda sucked."

"I'll get you more," I said, checking to see if her eyes were still closed. I kept tabs on her gown continuing to rise above her knees. I soon recognized the tiny dark brown mole on her thigh from that first night.

"You better fucking get me more." Her hair sprawled as her head was resting firmly against the couch's arm. "I'd love to go places, Julio." With her eyes still shut, her hand found her lips where she had drooled, and she ran her wrist across her mouth.

"Where?" I gently squeezed and pressed her feet, heel, ankle, and calves. Her bare knees kept slowly knocking against each other.

"Places. I would love to see places. Have you been places?"

"Just Puerto Rico and Ecuador."

"I would love to go to Puerto Rico. Mami says it's paradise." Squirming and then yawning. "I hate being by myself. I wish Usmaíl was here already so I'd have someone else. I would love to sing to the baby."

"You can sing—"

"I said to the baby, not you, okay?"

"Okay, fine," I said. And I don't know where I got the courage, but one hand left her foot and traced her tiny blue mole on her thigh. I brushed my fingers as if it could be erased. It was tiny and blue. Then, both my hands went back to her feet again. Taína's gown had finally risen all the way up past her full stomach. Her bra was decorated with pictures of the Tasmanian devil from Looney Tunes.

Taína must have felt the draft and quickly opened her eyes and pulled her gown down and straightened up a little, though she still lay on the couch like she was sunbathing, her feet at my lap. Taína licked her lips and stirred. She must have known I was looking, but she didn't seem to mind and didn't tell me anything.

"My thighs hurt, Julio." Eyes shut. "Rub my thighs."

And my heart jumped.

I slid my hands up Taína's thighs, gently, and I knew I would not be able to help myself as I felt wet and hot, and then I heard a voice coming from Taína's room.

"Peta Ponce, Peta Ponce, ayuda a mi nena," Doña Flores moaned.

Taína sprung quickly and, as best she could with her heavy body, lifted her legs away from me back to a sitting position. I straightened up, too, and placed my hands in front of me. Coming from Taína's bedroom, we heard Doña Flores talk in her sleep. *"Peta Ponce, por favor, dime, dime que pasó, Peta Ponce."* And then she crashed again.

We stayed silent for a minute.

All we could hear was the TV on low volume.

"My mother can't know you were here while she was

asleep." And she walked me to the door, but before ushering me out, Taína got on tippy toes and kissed my lips. It was a nice, slow kiss with no tongue, but a kiss. She then closed the door.

And I was left standing in a silent hallway. But that was okay. It was all okay, and it reminded me of my father sending that note to my mom: *When I saw you flowers started growing in my mind.*

MY MOTHER CAME along and she spoke for a long time. The doctor listened to all her venting. Then the doctor told my mother that what I was going through was nothing new. Many boys fall in love with pregnant women, he said. The marvelous gift to bring forth life. He said there were men who only liked looking at pregnant women. Men who got excited by it. The doctor went on and on, and my mother slapped my shoulder and interrupted him.

"Tell the doctor," she said, cutting him off, "tell him about your atom thing, tell him."

I repeated my theory of the subatomic pregnancy with a few new twists and turns. How in the darkness of inner space anything was possible.

"You do know that the atoms you were born with are all gone," the doctor said. "You are now made entirely out of new atoms?"

I knew this and nodded.

"Then how can an atom start a revolution when we lose atoms all the time?"

"Yes, it takes time, doesn't happen overnight, about a

year, maybe?" I said. "So this leaves the rebel atoms enough time to plant copies of themselves in the new cells that they created. Sort of like when a martyr is killed, but the revolution lives on and becomes even stronger."

"You do know"—the doctor frowned—"that this is highly unlikely."

"Yes but then," I said, "if we are made of atoms and all our original atoms are replaced by new atoms"—the doctor crossed his arms—"how can we still be us when all that we were, all our original matter has been replaced?" And he frowned as if he had never thought of that or as if he were bored.

The doctor sat back on his chair. He looked at Mom.

"Is he under any medication? Anything?" He was trying to show an interest in me, but I could tell he was now putting on a show for Mom.

"No," Mom said.

The doctor swiveled in his chair to face me again. He looked in my eyes and then faced my mother again. He told her it was nothing to worry about. That this wasn't psychotic behavior. I didn't speak of hurting myself or anyone else, and that I was just holding on to a crush or something and that he was a doctor and not a quantum physicist. It was something quite beautiful, he said. How the young can be so innocent in a very adult way. It was such a shame how as we grow up, we lose this. That is why, he continued, it is during this stage in puberty when the friends we make are the ones that we try to mold ourselves after. It was only when Mom sighed loudly that he stopped his lecturing.

The doctor asked me if I wanted my mother to leave the room. I said no and so he asked me point-blank.

"Have you tried drugs?"

"No," I said, which was true.

"Have you smoked pot?"

"Yes, once." I had forgotten that that was a drug, though I had never seen anyone die from a pot overdose. The other day BD had found a dime bag inside a Coke can by the gutter. It might have belonged to a dealer who was arrested on the street and didn't have time to get his pot back. So we smoked it. But it was only once, and we might have not even smoked it right because I didn't feel anything and just coughed a lot.

"Ay Jehovah," my mother whispered to herself. The doctor ignored her because he must have felt he was on to something.

"Then you have done drugs?"

"I guess." I shrugged, not wanting to face my mother, who was already thinking of what to say to my father, and more important to her elders, at the Kingdom Hall.

"Do you take alcohol? Do you drink?"

"No, but—"

"So you have tried alcohol?"

"No," I said.

Eventually the doctor stopped asking questions and silently reviewed my responses, which he had written down. Then he opened a drawer and brought out a Dixie Cup with the Simpsons cartoon on it. He didn't have to tell me anything. But he did.

"I need a sample."

I snatched the cup and breathed out hard like Taína does when she is bored or sick and tired of things.

Outside the doctor's office, Lincoln Hospital's psych ward was painted a soft pink like a day care center. Its tenth-floor visiting lounge had a huge window where patients got a great view of the New York skyline. Many patients found it beautiful. Many had pulled their chairs to face the large window. Or maybe the skyline reminded them of their lost freedom.

In the men's room I filled the cup and brought it back. The doctor repeated to Mom that it was nothing to worry about and that my urine sample would tell him the truth if I was doing drugs or not and, if I was doing drugs, what kinds of drugs I was taking. Depending on what the drug was, this might be the cause of my hallucinations. That's what he called them, hallucinations. And that if she was so worried, she could always make an appointment for me to see a specialist. And with that my mother was happy. Me? I was glad it was over and felt like I had gotten off easy.

Verse 9

I WAS ON my way to take some pictures for Sal when I spotted BD sitting on a housing project bench not far from the mailbox. The left sleeve of the Izod shirt I had bought him was dead limp. BD was crying, an angry, bitter cry. He was cursing to himself. He had been waiting for me.

"That motherfucker took it." He dry spat, his eyes had more water than his mouth. "Took my iPhone, too."

BD had been going around school wearing new clothes, iPhone, iPad, iPod Touch, and everyone had seen him at the latest movies, at Chipotle, Shake Shack, and showing off his leather jacket while counting his hundreds, living larger than a rapper.

"He wants a cut, Julio." Mario had beaten BD up because he would not tell him what our scam was.

"Okay, don't worry. First thing we got to get your arm back." Because I didn't know how much those things cost, but they must cost a lot and his mother would kill BD if he didn't come home with his arm.

"How?" BD wiped the tears from his face and spat some

phlegm and cleared his throat. "He wants five hundred for the arm."

"Let's just get your arm back," I said.

Mario lived on Pleasant Avenue in a nice tenement near a church. And while gentrification had tamed El Barrio, it could not rewrite its past. Pleasant Avenue is a six-block stretch that runs from 114th Street to 120th Street, just east of First Avenue. It's an Italian enclave shown in the movie *The Godfather*. The scene where Sonny Corleone beats up Carlo and leaves him bloodied by an opened fire hydrant. Italians and Puerto Ricans have been going at it since.

Things are much quieter now, but every once in a while someone like Mario De Puma shows up and bad blood starts up all over again, because like aluminum cans, the past is recyclable.

We reached Mario's door and knocked.

Mario's father opened. He was smoking a cigar and bopped his head as if to say, What you fellas want? He was a bigger, stronger version of Mario, with hands like milk crates. He could suffocate you with three fingers. Hairy knuckles stuck out like bedrock in Central Park.

"Mr. De Puma," I said nervously, "my friend is missing an arm and your son took it."

Mario's father looked at BD's limp sleeve.

He removed his cigar and laughed like Santa Claus.

"We just want the arm back, that's all." Making nothing of his laughing. But he couldn't stop.

"So let me get this straight," he said with no real Italian Hollywood movie accent, just a nasty brute voice, "your friend here got into a fight with Mario and couldn't protect himself?" He kept laughing. "And Mario took his fake shit arm?"

BD didn't say anything. I didn't say anything either.

"Now, whose fault is that?" he said, putting the cigar back in his mouth. Through the opened door I saw a fat lady ironing clothes in the living room. On the walls were pictures of her children. There was Mario as a little boy in a sailor outfit chasing ducks in Central Park. He looked nothing like the bully he was to become. There was also a cross and a picture of Brando, Sinatra, and DiMaggio, as well as snapshots of the pope.

The fat lady stopped ironing for a second and said, "Arm? What arm? Whose arm? Arm what?" She continued to iron. Mario's father turned toward her and told her what had happened.

The heavy lady didn't laugh. She kept ironing and then shrugged. "So, give him back the arm."

"No, no, wait, I asked these fellas a question," Mario's father said, turning back to us. "Because Mario is a man. I'm proud of my boy. A real man, that Mario." He looked at BD and me. "Actually we are all men here, right?" And only I nodded because BD had started to fade. His humiliation was growing. "Not pussies, right?" he said. "What's in it for me?" He put his cigar back in his mouth and crossed his arms.

"What you mean?" I said.

"If I give you back the arm, what?" He smoked away. Waiting for us to say something.

He took out his cigar, spat, and put it back in his mouth, holding it down with his side teeth.

"You know who my father was?" I didn't. BD was about to cry. "They called him Vinnie the Butcher. He owned the butcher shop on 119th Street and First. You know he never sold a single pork chop? The red stains on his apron never changed, they always stayed the same, because that shop was just his thing, you know, his thing, to make money." And he blew a lot of smoke in the air. "But you people arrived and ruined what was a once a great neighborhood. No one had to lock their doors on Pleasant Avenue before you people came." He crossed his arms and bobbed his head. "My father didn't have to sell a single pork chop because that shop was just his thing, but when you people came, your dumb mothers would walk in and ask for meat. Ask, why was there no meat? Ask, this is supposed to be a butcher shop and there was no meat? Your mothers made a big deal why was there no meat? You ruined his thing. You people ruin things and now you want your arm back!"

"That's not our fault, sir," I said respectfully, but he just got mad.

"What's not your fault, pussy?" He puffed away.

"What happened to your father." And BD tapped my arm with his good one, telling me we should just go. "Those mothers didn't know your father's shop was a front, they didn't understan—"

"What's there to understand? I don't like you people." He barked, "That's what's there to understand. Now you want your arm back? My son took that arm from you and like the pussies that you people are, you don't take it up with him but with me. You think that because I'm the father I'm going to be all soft?" he yelled, and the lady ironing left her duty and stomped over.

"What color is your arm? What it looks like?" she said to BD, a bit annoyed at having to leave her chores.

"It's an arm," BD whispered.

"What color?" she asked again.

BD silently stuck out his hand and showed her his brown skin. She exhaled inconveniently like this was a waste of her time and left to check her son's room.

Mario's father was fuming at us by the door, blaming all Puerto Ricans for destroying his past.

"Before you people arrived, we could leave our fire escape windows open all night, no gates before you arrived. You people steal. If I threw a coin in a fountain, you people grab it before it hits the water."

The lady returned with BD's arm.

"Go," she said, like shooing flies away with her hands. "Go, go. I have family to do." And she returned to her ironing. Mario's father spat some more tobacco and put the cigar back in his mouth before slamming the door.

Mario had written in big, bold, black letters FAGGOT on BD's arm.

"You can cover it with your shirtsleeve," I said to BD, who didn't say anything. "No one will see it, BD—see? The sleeve will cover it. We can try paint remover, okay?"

AT SCHOOL I did my best not to run into Mario. As long as there were people around I was fine. I had a meeting with old Mr. Gordon, the guidance counselor, about applying to colleges and all those financial aid junkets. Other than Princeton, I didn't really know which colleges to apply to since I really didn't know what I wanted to study. So like people who buy wines according to how pretty the label is, I asked him about schools that sounded kinda cool. I said Pepperdine because it sounded like a character from *Peanuts*. Mr. Gordon laughed. He shook his head and said that I would never get in. Okay, what about Duke? Nope, he said, never get in. Vanderbilt, sound good? Nope, never get in. Bowdoin? Nope, never get in. Pomona? Nope, never get in. Swarthmore? Nope, never get in. Yale, sounds like jail? Absolutely not, he said, never, ever get in. Cornell? Nope. Dartmouth, funny name? Nope. Princeton? Never in a million years get in. When I said Harvard, he stopped me and gave me a long list. Told me to google these schools' admissions pages and that I should be fine.

A little later I was walking in the hallway, avoiding Mario at all costs, reading the list of colleges, when Ms. Cahill saw me and asked what I was reading so intensely.

"That's it?" She frowned. "Only community colleges?"

"He said that even if I make it into the private schools, I would be in debt all my life." Sounded wrong to me, but I had been taught to respect my elders in public and trash them behind their backs, so I'd stayed quiet when he told me this.

Ms. Cahill blew an angry loose strand of hair away and led me to her empty classroom. She closed the door and asked me to sit by her desk.

"Where would you like to apply?" she asked.

"Princeton"—because I knew Einstein taught there—

"though I don't know if I want to study science. I like it, but I don't know. I could also live at home and cut costs."

"That's a great idea and great choice," she said, and then lowered her voice, though it was just us in that classroom. "There are some teachers"—she said this carefully, but I knew whom she was referring to—"who come from a different era. Who have been teaching here since the 1900s and think like we are still living in the 1900s, too. Now, I read your college essay, Julio." And she fondled through a mess of paper on top of her desk and found it. "It was excellent. It's what colleges look for, Julio. People who help others. And you wrote it in a creative, concise, and precise, grammatically correct structure. Did you really befriend this ex-convict, really?"

"Yeah," I said. "But the essay is not finished."

"Good," she said. "Please finish it and show it to me before you send all your stuff out. Listen, Julio, your grades and your AP scores are also good. Not excellent, but good—" Her iPhone on the desk vibrated. The screen showed a picture of a cop, only his shirt was undone, exposing his bare chest. Ms. Cahill quickly answered it and said to call her later.

"Yeah, okay," I said, "but I don't want to get into debt, either."

"Listen, I know scholarships are hard to come by. I myself did not get one. All I can tell you is . . ." And she thought for a second how to word this. I think she was trying to find something specific within my life so as to use that as her base. "You go to church, am I right?"

"I used to," I say, "but yeah, sure."

"Okay, listen, I think you heard the saying, I think it's in the Good Book, that says if you don't work, you don't eat. Am I right?"

"It's Paul," I said. "My father, who's a communist, told me that Lenin used it, too. Weird, huh, Ms. Cahill?"

"No, not at all. Christianity and communism aren't all that different." And just when she was going to continue, her iPhone rang again. On the screen was a picture of different cop, only this one had no shirt or anything. He was completely nude, letting the taco fly with only his cop hat on. Ms. Cahill tried to turn it off before I could see it, but I played it off. "What I need to tell you is, listen, there are people who are born with bread and never have to work. There are people who inherit bread, their uncle dies and leaves them money or parents die and leave them money. There are people who win bread, they hit the lottery or some sweepstakes. The saddest and most unfair part of that phrase, Julio, is that there are people who work very hard under the sun like migrant workers do picking strawberries or lettuce and they receive very little or no bread."

"I get your point," I said, but I wanted to ask her about Taína, about the day she sang. I knew she had been present. But I let her finish.

"Great, Julio, because what no one can inherit, win, find, or work for, is . . . more . . . time. Time is the real gold. Not money. Time is the gold. It's what you do with your time that matters. So if you want to apply to Princeton, I will help you. You have a shot. Debt or no debt, you would have used your time well in reaching for what you want, and it's a great thing."

She held my eyes for a second. I didn't tell her that I knew old Mr. Gordon was full of shit.

"Ms. Cahill," I said, "can I ask you something that has nothing to do with this?"

"Ah, ah, ah, sure," she said nervously, because she knew all the boys liked her. I think she knew she was gorgeous, and this can be a frightening thing, I think. Taína didn't know she was gorgeous.

"You remember Taína?"

"Taína? . . . Taína? Oh, that girl. Such a sad thing." Her tone changed, like she was talking about a hurt puppy. "So, so sad."

"She once sang in the music room. You were there, right?"

"Was I?"

"I've heard you said that everyone saw whom they loved and who loved them back. Is this true?"

She focused her eyes somewhere else and thought about this for a second. Her eyebrows wrinkled and then she opened her mouth a bit and said, "Ah, yes, I do remember her singing. Lovely, lovely voice. Truly lovely."

"Well, is it true that you saw people you love?"

"Are you serious?"

"Yeah, I heard that you said that."

"Well, maybe I did at that time, but what I recall . . ." Pausing, scanning her memory. "What stands out was how Mario, you know Mario? Everyone knows Mario. How he was so taken by her singing he sort of shriveled up in his chair."

"Mario?!!!"

"It was a bit funny how this tough guy was moved by her singing and just melted." She laughed a little laugh.

"Mario?!!!"

"Yes, Mario. Before she stopped attending, I thought they were a couple because when I'd see them, they were not far from each other. That's you kids and love. I throw no stones, I love, love." She smiled. "I love, love. Love it."

"Mario?"

"Yes."

"No fucking way!!!"

Verse 10

I WENT TO take some pictures. I arrived at the Capeman's playground. It was drenched in sunlight and color. There was a big blue sign graffitied on the handball court: IF YOU GENTRIFY, THEY WILL COME. In Salvador's days, this part of the city was called Hell's Kitchen. It was full of greasy diners, prostitutes, pimps, hustlers, and junkies, as well as hardworking people and their families who went about their business living in affordable apartments. The playground had been remodeled, surrounded by a new and shiny white wired fence. There were fresh wooden benches lining both sides of the playground. Right in the middle, like an island, was a little, vibrantly painted storehouse where the custodians kept their brooms and cleaning stuff. There was a fresh sandbox and a long silver slide next to a row of metal swings. It was here, on the swings, where the two boys and their friends were just innocently shooting the breeze before the Capeman and his Vampires arrived. I walked a little farther up and took pictures of the Sixteenth Precinct on West 47th where the Capeman had been booked. I had bought Sal a camera as a gift and was shooting pictures in the daytime so he could see these places in sunlight. I planned on giving him the camera and the pictures so that maybe he might want to go out in the daytime and shoot pictures one day.

Back home, I turned on my laptop and googled the bejesus out of Sal. Everything I could find. All his life as the Capeman and a bit after. I sat on my bed and read, doing research and taking notes for my college essay:

> *Salvador Negron was 16 when he was tried as an adult in the last year of the doo-wop 1950s. He was the youngest ever to be sentenced to death by electric chair. For two years death slept, ate, and breathed with him, and laughed at him, until that fateful day. For his last meal, he had ordered Puerto Rican dishes: pernil, arroz con gandulez, flan, and a tall glass of maví. But all he got was fried chicken, mashed potatoes, green peas, garlic bread, and apple pie. He ate his last meal sadly, but he was happy that he might see heaven in a couple of hours. Afterward, when his name and number were called, "On the gate!" he fainted. When he opened his eyes, he was not in heaven, or strapped to a chair, but rather back in his cell courtesy of a last-second pardon by Nelson Rockefeller, who was governor of New York.*

I stopped reading. All I could think of was that first day I met him. How he reminded me of an old broken-down Jesus Christ, whose disciples had long ago deserted him.

Verse 11

TAÍNA OPENED THE door. She held a finger to her lips. "Mami is asleep in my room again," she whispered. "Don't make a sound, dummy." And I angrily tiptoed inside. I could see that Doña Flores talked in her sleep as she snored a ghost story. We sat on the couch. I felt Taína's warmth as hot as my anger. Taína was wearing the same see-through gown, though this time she had not thrown a T-shirt over it—and those colors arrived. I saw red circles doing circles inside blue circles inside white circles and my heart was pounding to those circles.

"It's sausage, mushrooms, and peppers, you better like them," I said, trying not to look. "I wasn't sure what you wanted so I just picked these. If you don't like them it's too bad." But I gave myself away and Taína knew I was looking at her breasts and crossed her arms. "And oh, I got you gum." I folded. I tried to be nice, even though I was still angry.

Taína, who had made a big stink about wanting gum,

didn't take the gum. Instead she went for the pizza. She sat on the couch.

"This pizza sucks," she said, continuing to eat, "horrible pizza." And soon she picked up another slice. "Terrible, where you get this shit pizza? I should starve before I eat this crap." But she kept eating.

I pretended to watch television, a Pixar movie at low volume. I wanted to kiss her like before. Pick up where we had left off. But Mario hung in the room.

"Next time bring some Coke. Who brings pizza with nothing to drink?" She ordered me to get her something to drink from the kitchen. She said that really loudly, even though when I first walked in she had told me to be quiet. "And I don't want orange juice," she yelled from the living room. And Doña Flores slept like a rock.

But there was nothing to drink in her almost empty fridge but orange juice and milk.

When I brought her a glass of milk, she made a face.

"Are you fucking retarded?"

"That's all you have," I said, "and you said you don't want orange juice."

"So get me water, then, jeez. Can you do that? Can you?"

So I got her water.

"'Bout time," she said, and took a sip.

I was hungry, but I didn't eat anything and let her have as many slices as she wanted. I enjoyed watching her eat. I liked the way her lips shone from the pizza's grease and how her temples went up and down as she chewed. I could understand why any guy would fall for her.

When my mother had to say something to me that she didn't want to talk about, she would just say it. She would come out and set it free without thinking, like jumping into cold water. Straight up.

"Mario." If I stayed calm and didn't get myself pissed off and concentrated, I wouldn't yell, I thought.

"Mario who? Mario what?" She shrugged.

"Mario, from school. I'm sure you know him."

"Who again?"

"Mario, Italian guy. Big with muscles and nothing up there."

"Oh, that guy?" she said.

"Yeah," I said, "that guy."

"He was nice."

"What?"

"No, he was one of the few who never said anything mean to me. He would leave me cannoli on my desk, I'm serious."

She must have seen my angry nostrils or heard my heart beating like a conga. She smiled and lifted her head as if she now knew what this was all about. Why I was mad at her.

"Ya sé qué bicho te picó." She shook her head. "You men all the same."

"I'm leaving," I said.

"That'll be your fucking loss," she said loudly. "Because nothing happened."

I didn't leave, but I couldn't look at her either. I gave her my back. Her bedroom door in front of me was wide-open. Doña Flores was stiff. If she weren't making noises or talking in her sleep, you'd think she was dead. Her body lay facing the ceiling. Her hands lay folded on top of her chest and she was wearing a nice blue dress, as if she had just come back from a party or as if this was her funeral bed.

Taína turned me around. We came face-to-face. She saw my unhappiness. For once Taína looked more nervous than me. For a second she played with a strand of hair before tugging it behind her lovely left ear. She licked her lips and gently pushed me to sit on the couch. She then gently sat her pregnant body next to me.

"You know that your mother left my mother flat?"

"Yeah, I know."

"Just when my mom needed her support."

"Yeah, I know."

"I won't call your mother a bitch only cuz I know you. So you know, with her best friend gone and shit, my mother met this guy. My good-for-nothing father, who was one of those Latinos who fucking hates other Latinos." Her tone was soft, but the color was still there.

"I heard," I said. "Your uncle Sal told me. What does this have to do with Mario?"

Taína paused. Her angry eyes told me not to interrupt her again.

"If you fucking let me talk, bitch . . . I will tell you. God. . . . Mami was pregnant with me and all she'd hear from him was how Latinos hate each other. He blamed all Latinos for him growing up in the South Bronx, for his father's shit job at a factory, for his mother's shit Social Security checks, he blamed Latinos for where he lived with Mami, for this shit housing project, for any shit he'd blame

Latinos. Especially Puerto Ricans, which he was but he hated them more than anyone. He said that we had been in this shit country before the other Latinos arrived and we hadn't done shit. That Mexicans had taken over California and that Cubans owned Miami, and that even those fucking Koreans had cornered the vegetable market stands, but Puerto Ricans had done shit. He used to work at a bank in midtown, Mami told me, that's where they met. She had to cash her receptionist checks there. He was a good teller, from what Mami tells me he was great with numbers. I hate fucking numbers, so I'm happy I inherited shit from him. But he loved working with white people at that bank. He was going to night school in trying to better himself, too, Mami said, but one day when a promotion was due to him, they passed him over and gave it to a black guy." She paused and saw how mad I was. "Jeez, it's hard to tell you this when you look like I killed your fucking dog—"

"What does this have to do with Mario?" I did my best to breathe silently.

"I swear to God if you say that again before letting me finish, I will bitch-slap your fucking face so har—"

"Fine, finish."

"My good-for-nothing father was okay with this black guy getting the promotion. Until he found out that that bank manager who spoke great English and had gone to college was not a fucking white guy but Dominican. A fucking white-skin Dominican in charge of everyone in that bank. All of a sudden it was how that fucking white Dominican had kept him down. Latinos, he would say, we hold each other down in water so we can drown. He was fired and never came home. That fuck left Mami with me still inside. This is what Mami tells me. I never saw him, never met the fuck. I hope he's dead. I hope he fuckin—"

"Mario," I said, "did—"

"Hold your horses, I'm trying to explain this shit. So when I was like eleven and knew that guys were looking at my ass, you know, when I knew this I steered away from Latinos. So when at school an Italian guy liked me, you know, brought me cannoli, I thought, Okay, he's not Latino. This is okay, you know, this is good? And you"—she poked at my arm—"you were cute but Latino and never said shit to me, you were like chickenshit scared or a big wuss."

"You think I'm cute?"

Taína just smiled and exhaled. I did not mention to her that Italians were Latins because I kind of understood where she was coming from. Her father was ugly, and he had been raised during a time in the South Bronx when vacant lots grew like toxic gardens. He'd grown up surrounded by street boys that if caught stealing they'd lie, if beaten they'd curse, if sent to prison they'd go kicking and screaming, blaming the world for hating them. I could only think that Taína's father had tried hard to avoid being like them. Though he had not ended up dead or in prison, they had already infected him. He was a carrier of the ghetto. So why would I blame Taína? She was defending herself as best she could from the same brutality I was trying to dodge. Didn't mean I had to like it, though.

"Before Mami yanked me out of school, I remember sitting on a bench in the schoolyard all by myself because no one would sit next to me. Not even you—"

"I was scared of you," I whispered. "You're right, I was scared, you were so pretty."

"What? Speak up, bitch. I was what?"

"Nothing." But I think she had heard me.

"Fine." She studied my face for a second and continued. "He came over and sat right next to me. I will not lie to you, I liked that he sat next to me."

"Oh, gaaad." I was like puking.

"No, really. I sensed that he wanted to talk to me. To be nice to me, he just didn't fucking know how to do it. You know, the way that I can't help but to curse. And then he saw his boys coming out of the school doors. I know how you boys get when your boys show up, it's like now you have to put on a show because if—"

"What happened?"

"Fuck you. Fine. Nothing happened. Didn't say a fucking word, he left a cannoli on the bench and went over to his boys, lighting a cigarette, like I never existed. From that day on, he'd always leave them for me."

"Always?"

"Yeah. He knew where I sat and my schedule and leave fresh cannoli in a plastic bag inside my desk."

"And what you do?"

"I fucking ate them. What you think? Those shits are good."

Taína got really close to me and held my hands.

"Nothing ever happened."

"Nothing?"

"On my baby's life, okay?" When she said that, I believed her. "We good?" she said. I stayed quiet because half of me didn't blame Mario, Taína was lovely, but the other half wanted to get back at him, though I didn't know how.

"We good? Or what? The fuck?"

I nodded. I could never stay mad at Taína.

"Good. I want to show you something," Taína whispered. She rarely whispered. "I love my iPod. I listen to it, but only at night," she said, and we got up from the couch. I helped bring her pregnant body up only weeks before the arrival. She guided me to the living room closet door.

"Don't tell my mother ever or I'll fucking kill you till you're dead." She opened the closet door. The shelves and the closet floor were overflowing with children's musical instruments. There was a baby maraca, a baby trumpet, small bongos and a drum, a ukulele, a little kid's piano, and a small keyboard whose batteries were long dead.

"You can play all these?" I asked, but she didn't answer me.

There were musical awards and certificates from P.S. 72 that Taína had won and tons of pictures of her singing as a little kid. I picked one up. A seven-year-old Taína in jeans and a Winnie-the-Pooh T-shirt, standing in front of a microphone bigger than her whole face.

"Shit, give me that." She snatched it away from me.

"Can I see it?"

"No," she said defensively. "My mother never bought me toys. What little money she had was spent on instruments, for fuck's sake."

"Can you play them?"

"Yeah, I can play them, okay? Jeez. It's not what I want to show you, okay." She pointed at the top shelf. "Bring those down," she ordered me, because she couldn't reach that high.

The top shelf was loaded with piles and piles of records in all three speeds: 78, 33⅓, and 45 rpm. Ray Barretto's *Señor 007,* Willie Colón's *Cosa Nuestra* and *Lo Mato,* Celia Cruz's *Homenaje a los Santos* and *Azucar Negra,* Ismael *"el Sonero Mayor"* Rivera's *Fiesta Boricua,* El Gran Combo, Rubén Blades, and older albums of stars like Los Panchos, Xavier Cugat, Israel Fajardo, Tito Puente, Miguelito Valdéz, Ramón *"el Jamón"* Ortiz, Machito, La Lupe, and Iris Chacón, and Cesar and Nestor Castillo's award-winning album *The Mambo Kings Play Songs of Love.* And with some effort, as it was at the bottom of a heavy pile that I had brought down, Taína showed me Héctor Lavoe's little-known album, *La Plancha.*

"That's your mom, right?"

I held an old LP, a 33⅓. This absurdly gorgeous, smiling, teenage bottle blonde with violet-colored contact lenses and olive skin lay on an ironing board in her bra and tiny panties. Behind her, Héctor Lavoe and the band were going to make her wrinkle free as they held red-hot irons in their hands.

"She's pretty," Taína said.

"Pretty fake," I said.

"All girls are fake, you stupid idiot," she said. "We wear makeup, heels, and all kinds of shit."

We heard Doña Flores stir. Talking to herself or the walls about Peta Ponce. Asking her questions.

Taína took the record away from me. We put everything back as quickly as possible and closed the closet.

She led me to the door.

"Peta Ponce, you gonna be there, right?"

"Of course," I said, and for a moment I thought she was going to kiss me like the last time. I shifted my body and placed my face in front of hers.

"Don't forget to bring soda next time," she said. "Who eats fucking pizza without soda?" And she closed the door.

It had not been a good night. Taína had given Mario a chance; she might have even liked him. And she didn't kiss me good-bye. I thought how cruel the gods are. Here is eternal life, but not eternal youth. Here is the power to predict the future, but no one will believe you. Here is a picture of a hot girl in bra and panties, but it's your mother. And Taína had not kissed me.

Verse 12

"I THINK YOUR mother is mad at me and I want to cook something really good for her," my father said in Spanish. He asked me if I could lend him a hundred dollars. I thought it a great, great idea.

"That *seco de chivo* you made the other day wasn't that bad, Pa." I had tried it and liked it, though Mom didn't take a single bite, and to show how disgusted she was, she left the house and came back with a Big Mac.

"I want to get some flowers, a *pernil* to bake, a bottle of Chivas—your mother likes Chivas—an old record, I do not know which one yet, and a new pair of shoes, too."

"You know her size?"

"No, but I will bring a shoe with me to the store." And as he kept talking I realized he was doing this not because he was apologizing or anything, he was doing this because it was going to be my mother's birthday. Like all Jehovah's Witnesses, my mother doesn't celebrate birthdays. Hers, my father's, mine, or anybody's. But this never stopped him from throwing her or me a little party anyway. When he did have a job and it was my birthday, he'd take me to a movie or to the bleachers at Yankee Stadium. For my mother, though, he'd wrap presents on purpose because as a Jehovah's Witness, Mom wasn't supposed to receive gifts on that day. But he'd wrap them, knowing that Mom's curiosity would get the best of her. She always protested. Asking her God for forgiveness. But in the end she always caved.

"I'll even serve her," Pops said.

"*Sí, claro, Pa,* I have a hundred dollars for you." I had just taken a dog back and I was flush. Though most of that money was going to Doña Flores, because Salvador had told me that Peta Ponce was coming from Puerto Rico in a day or two. Taína wanted me to be there, and no matter what, not angels or demons were going to stop me from being near Taína when the *espiritista* arrived at her house.

"You know I am proud of you." My father squeezed my shoulder, and it made me happy. It had nothing to do with money. It had to do with him being able to ask me without any embarrassment. I wished that Mom could be a little bit like that. But Mom was very closed. She would rather hide things behind anger or sarcasm.

"I will find a job and pay you back."

"You know Pa"—because he was my dad and I owed him more than money—"you do have a job, you cook and clean and you always walk my dogs and feed them and stuff."

"No, no, no," he said firmly. "I like walking your dogs. I only clean and cook to keep my own conscience clear until I get a job." But he had always been chronically unemployed. As soon as he'd find a job, he'd lose it in no time. Always blaming authority, how bosses should not exist at all. How the camaraderie of the rich is built on the fear that the day will come when the poor will grow so desperate they will knock down the wealthy's doors and rush uninvited, plundering their wealth and dirtying up their Persian rugs. How things in his native Ecuador were better and how Marxism is the answer. And blah, blah, blah, just like Mom with her Jehovah, Marx's words were his law. And soon, he'd bore everyone at work until they grew so sick and tired of him, he was fired. I think that was another reason why Mom was angry a lot. She felt pressed. I'm not blaming my father. I'm just trying to better understand Mom. All this responsibility of keeping the refrigerator full falling on her.

"Pa," I said, resting my hand on his shoulder, which I rarely do, *"usted sabe que Mami lo hizo. ¿Verdad?"* I said in Spanish, because adding that to touching his shoulder meant I wanted to talk to him about something important.

"Did what?" he said in Spanish, like I was asking him to buy toothpaste.

"Mami lo hizo, ¿usted sabe?" And I tried to hold his eyes, but he was more interested in vacuuming soon.

"No. Tell me, did what? Tell me." He was more lost than Columbus.

"La operación," I said.

And that word made him freeze and clam up.

"Just tell me," I said in a low, respectful voice, "whatever you want to tell me, Pa. It's okay. And if you don't want to tell me anything, that is okay, too."

He cleared his throat. He shuffled his feet like a boxer.

Put his hands in his pocket and then took them back out. Licked his lips and didn't know where to start.

"Do not think that I do not love you," he said, clearing his throat some more.

"I know, Pa."

"Do not think I do not love your mother."

"I know."

"I did not know the language at all. I did not know anything. I had been here less than a year when that happened." He shook his head like he still couldn't believe it. "The doctors talked to me. They told me this was best. I would not have agreed, but, but, but I did not understand. I was new here."

"But, Pa," I said. "Mom knows English. She must have known what they wanted to do to her? She must have translated to you?"

"Do not blame your mother. She had just given birth to you," he said, and I had never seen my father this close to crying. "She comes from a culture where this is nothing. So many do it. So many were forced to do it that it becomes nothing. All I know is she never blamed me for anything. And I will not blame her, too."

"Okay. I'm fine with that," I said.

"All I remember was you. You cried so loud and later I held you. Your mother did not tell me anything till later. She cried a lot and she became closer to her God. And I let her because if that is what it took, then that is what it took to make her not feel guilty," he said, more composed but still needing to clear his running throat.

"What about Peta Ponce?"

"Enough. Enough," he said, tired. "That crazy woman? Are we not men, Julio?" he said, as if men are not supposed to talk about these issues. "Men. We are men. Right, son?" My father was from a different time, a different country, a communist philosophy. Like him not blaming my mother and like her not blaming him, I could not blame my father for his way of thinking or try to change him. Though he himself had told me that as men, we should never run from anything. That whatever you ran away from would one day come back stronger than you and armed to the teeth. And now, he was not taking his own advice. But he had said enough and there was no point in making him angry. If another time showed itself to talk, then fine. If not, fine, too. But we had discussed it. The secrets between us two were no longer valid.

"Yeah, Pa," I said, "we are men." Because that's what he wanted to hear. I gave him another hug. He put the money I had given him in his pocket and quickly went to vacuum the living room.

I GAVE SALVADOR the camera. He held it in his hands as if thinking of selling it. But when I told him what was in the envelope he almost snatched it away. "In the daytime?" He didn't wait for my response. He quickly took the pictures out of the envelope. He began to study them like he was searching for Waldo. His mouth was half-open, and never did the old man smile. It was more like he was in awe of the daylight. I had gone to see him early, like eight thirty, because I wanted him to come and walk with me. Maybe even convince Taína and his sister to come out this early in the nighttime and take a stroll.

"You know, we can talk by the East River," I said. "It's nice there."

"Man, I wish I had a magnifying glass," he said to himself, and continued to study his pictures. He squinted. His eyes became insect slants.

"We can go buy one," I said. "I bet the Duane Reade has one."

"What?"

"We can buy one, man. Let's go get Taína and her mother and go buy one, Sal."

"Nah." He held the picture of the playground up to the light. "Nah, I need to look at this right now, *papo*."

I left him alone and leaned against the old piano. I looked at his *vejigante* costume hanging by the closet door, bright colors dominating everything in the tiny apartment. I asked him if he'd wear it tonight. But he was transfixed. I didn't exist. He mumbled little words to himself and then nodded. He was happy, I think, but in a way I could not figure out. When he held the picture of the playground, he took a step backward. He stared at the wall and back at the picture, and then he looked back at me.

"You sure this is the same place? It don't look like it."

"It's the same place, Sal."

"Damn, see, I've never seen it like this. Never seen it with this much light. It looks like a real playground. Let's go there now, right now, *papo*."

"The playground?"

"The playground."

"You serious!"

"Yeah, now." The playground was calling him. The old man put on his shoes and then his cape and grabbed his walking stick. I let everything I wanted to talk about drop; there would be another time. I looked forward to being somewhere other than this basement.

"You got subway fare for me, right, *papo*?"

"I got better," I said. "Let's cab it."

Salvador brought the pictures, and during the cab ride he didn't say anything. He kept staring out the window, watching Spanish Harlem flash by. He had lived in many places, on different blocks. He had sung doo-wop on countless street corners, and looking out the cab window was doing things to his memories. We crossed Central Park and drove toward the Upper West Side and then toward Clinton.

We arrived at West 46th and Ninth Avenue. I paid the driver and Salvador jumped out of the cab like he was on fire. He ran to the fence and took the picture of the playground out of the envelope. He compared the real playground with the picture. Salvador didn't enter the playground. He walked around the fenced playground and his memories were running backward. He placed his hands on the steel wires and screamed like he wanted to bring the fence down.

I sensed his embarrassment. His shame at having me witness him yell like that. And then he became a docile old man again.

"You know, *papo,* if I could, all I would ask is to start again. That's all I want, to start again. But you can't do that, *papo*." He had told me this once before. "But if I could start"—I could tell he had had this conversation with himself many times—"where would I start?" He looked at the picture again. "My life was a mess from day one. Where would I start?"

"You can start now? Today," I said. "You know, Sal, you shouldn't punish yourself more than you already have by living in the dark."

"I have to." He put the picture away and began walking toward the precinct.

"No, you don't. Listen, man, you don't have to feel shame, you paid your dues, you were locked up for decades—"

"Didn't bring anybody back," he cut me off in a firm but polite manner. I finally saw a half smile, though it was more out of sadness than anything.

We walked through Salvador's Hell's Kitchen. The rough neighborhood where the Marvel Comics street-savvy Irish superhero Daredevil was from. But gentrification had turned Hell's Kitchen into Clinton, and the only thing hellish about that neighborhood now was its rents.

"Mira, papo, you ever heard that story about Destiny coming to play cards with this bum?" I shook my head. "Well, Destiny comes to play cards and the bum thinks he can win and change his future. But see, *papo,* the bum sees that Destiny cheats. The bum sees all the rotten things Destiny does and so the bum loses. Destiny says to the bum, You'll always be a bum. The bum says, Because you cheat. And Destiny says, Yeah, but I let you play."

"I don't get it," I said.

"Means I had a rotten life from the start," he said, "but

at least I was given one. And maybe that's it. I don't know? Maybe even with my rotten life I should be happy. Right? But this makes little sense, *papo*."

"You know, Sal, maybe this *espiritista* can help you, too. Peta Ponce, I mean. She's coming anyway, can't hurt."

But he kept walking.

When we reached the precinct, he didn't go in. Just as with the playground, he compared the real with the picture.

"Sal," I said, "I know the daylight does things to you, but what if I come with you to these places in the daylight? You know, so you won't be alone?"

"No, *papo*," he said, staring at the precinct. "In the daytime I might bump into one of them."

"Bump into who?"

"The mothers."

"The mothers? What mothers?"

"The mother of one of the boys," he said, as if it were obvious.

This was very, very unlikely, I thought. It had happened so long ago, those mothers must be dust. The decade of the Capeman had died, too. Most people who were grown adults from that time had left to the stars. But he held on that this was not the case. If he was still walking the earth, these women were, too.

"Sal, the chances of you running into one of them are like, zero."

"No, *papo*." He shook his head really fast. "The mothers are here. Right now. Somewhere sleeping." His eyes scanned the newly renovated tenements and town houses now worth millions that stood across from us. "And if I run into them, what would I tell her? How could I explain that I took their sons away? You know, *papo*?"

It was more than the daylight shaming him. It was about him facing a dead past in real people. Even if one of those mothers were alive and by chance he'd run into one of them, she'd never recognize him or he her. But Salvador believed in his heart that this encounter was sure to happen. In his head existed living ghosts.

"We could go to those boys' graves, at night," I said.

"What for?" He took his eyes off the precinct and placed them on me.

"To say you're sorry."

And his face swelled up. Even at night I could see the pools in his eyes starting to fill up. Salvador never made noise when he cried. He didn't even sniffle, he just wept silent tears that clogged in his crow's-feet. They sat there stuck on his wrinkled face like crusty memories.

"That's for the living. Visiting graves is for the living, *papo*. I can't say sorry to the dead." His voice not cracking, just tears. And then slowly he walked up the stairs of the precinct and opened the door.

"Exactly," I said. "It's to make you feel better. You're still alive. It's for you."

"Me? That's not important, those boys are. And it's too late."

I thought he was going to go inside, but he closed the door.

"They brought me out in cuffs," he said, walking back down the stairs, wiping his tears but not his sadness. "There were a lot of people outside, television, camera crews, lights, reporters. All blocking the way to the cop car that was going to take me to the Tombs." And he showed me where the television crews had lined the sidewalk. Then he stopped just right at the edge of the curb. "This reporter shoved a microphone in my face. I had seen him before, he wore glasses, from Channel Four, named Gabe Pressman, and he was the one who asked me, 'How do you think your mother feels right now?' " And his eyes continued drooling, but he could talk without choking up. "That's when I said it." Like the daylight, it shamed him. "That's when I said that thing, you know, *papo,* the thing, those words. I was a kid. I saw all those lights and they made me feel big and bad. Like a movie star. I was a kid. So I said it, but I was just a kid. They called me the Cape*man*, but I was a kid. So I said it, I said, 'I don't care if I burn. My mother can watch.' "

"It's all right, Sal," I said, though I could never really know what it must be like to live in his shoes. To understand his guilt for things he could not take back. There was nothing he could do or say. His life was the moral. Salvador was stuck with that life, and whether others learned from it or not, whether he had been forgiven or not, there was no reset button. A life with no rehearsal. The actor goes onstage cold and with no script.

"I never meant to say that about my mother, *papo*."

"I know, Sal."

"You know, she died while I was in that place." He meant prison, I knew. "So I never got a chance to say to Mom that I was sorry."

It was cruel arithmetic, like that guy from Greek myths who rolls the rock up a hill only to have it come tumbling down again. Sal was that guy. Sal was Sisyphus. He didn't complain or say it was unfair, he just took it. Though it hurt him, made him sad and shameful, he accepted that he had done terrible things and felt it was only just he should suffer. He made suffering his thing. He played and replayed that night's events in his mind endless times, and each time he was the killer.

"All I would ask is to start again." But this time he didn't finish the sentence. His shoulders slumped and his old gangly arms drooped to his side. Sal's long, thin frame hung lifeless, the way his costume did in his apartment. I tried to place my arm around el Vejigante, but I couldn't reach his shoulder. He was too tall, so I planted my hand flat on his back and patted the crying old man.

"It's all right, Sal." I patted the old man like I was burping a baby. "It's all right. It's all right, man. It's all right."

Verse 13

I ENTERED MY project building. The elevator door opened to Mario waiting. He quickly put me in a headlock. He dragged me inside the elevator. He punched me in the face, then punched the last floor on the elevator and dragged me to the roof. The night sky was beautiful. Freshly washed laundry was drying on clotheslines not far from our project building. The white sheets swirled in the wind, and the New York skyline glowed in all its glory.

"If I remember right, you and that cripple used to only wear Skechers, now I see you wear Nikes," Mario said after throwing me on the asphalt.

"Listen, Mario, we can talk. Okay? We can find a way to work this out," I said, hoping he was not crazy enough to throw me over the roof like cops would do to Puerto Ricans back in the day. Maybe even still today.

He punched my face.

I got back up.

"Mario, can we talk?" I thought about what Taína had told me. I tried to see him in a different light. Maybe he was just putting on a show for his boys and was really not that bad of a guy. I myself had been guilty of that, too. I had lied in front of my friends and had done things that I was not proud of to look cool in their eyes.

"Listen, Mario, I have an idea—"

Mario punched me in the stomach.

I was back on the ground.

"I took your friend's arm, but, okay, but he got that shit back. Now tell me, what's your hustle?"

I looked up at Mario, and for the life of me I could not see the guy who brought Taína cannoli. The guy she told was sweet to her was nowhere on that roof. He grabbed me by my shirt and lifted me up from the ground with no problem.

"You always got money. What's your hustle?"

He let go of my shirt so I could tell him. "How the fuck you get the money?" he shouted.

I was on top of a roof, high in the sky, closer to God. But I knew God was not going to come save me.

"What's your hustle, psycho, and don't tell me it's an ancient Chinese secret," he spat.

"Mario, why you gotta be like this?" I said in pain. "Taína told me you brought her pastries—"

I got decked on the side of my face.

"Wha?"

"You were nice to her?" I coughed.

"Bitch is lying!" he yelled. "I never brought her cannoli."

"See! I never said they were cannoli! So how you kno—"

I got decked again.

I flung my body headfirst toward Mario to maybe bring

him down, but he just tossed me aside like a wafer. I landed on my back. I could see the moon was full. There was a dark blue cloud in the shape of a bird.

"Fuck that bitch. She was all big tits and nothing else." And I wished Taína were here so she could see him the way I saw him. Still, I tried to reason with him and decided not to fight anymore.

"Okay," I said, "but you have to work with us. I'll cut you in, okay?"

"Work? Whachoo mean work? You work. If your thing is work, I'll just tax you."

He slapped my face and then dared me to fight back.

I did not move.

He waited. He was angrier than I was because I was not saying anything.

"I'm taxing you. One hundred a month."

I couldn't help myself and cursed at him. Bad move. He punched me in the gut. As I doubled over in pain, he dug inside my jeans and robbed me. He counted the bills and liked what he saw. "Inflation," he said, happy with the money, "two hundred a month."

I stayed quiet more out of pain. "This is back pay," he said, showing me my own bills that were now his. "First payment is next month. Or this time I'm not taking BD's arm but yours."

Mario talked and threatened like the worst of what Pleasant Avenue was when it was still called Little Italy, past mobsters who swindled those who couldn't go to the cops. Those like me who were swindling someone else. I thought about Mario and me being infected with the same brutal violence of our neighborhood, but I was in too much pain to try to come to an understanding of it.

Mario split.

I was happy to see him go. My stomach felt like I had eaten rocks. I sat on the tar roof fourteen floors up and wished I could jump to the tenement that loomed ahead. Land by the clotheslines and unhook a clean white sheet to wrap myself with. Shivering with humiliation, I watched the New York skyline. I thought New York City was choking itself to death. Too many ugly, cheap skyscrapers were being built, and the skyline was now a mess of cluttered rectangles. Beauties like the Chrysler building needed their own space, their own stage to shine. Instead it was being squeezed, smothered, and smashed by the other shit skyscrapers. You could no longer make out the gargoyles. The world's greatest skyline had been crushed into a bunch of tightly compressed shit boxes.

THE FOURTH BOOK OF JULIO

PETA PONCE

There are spirits who aren't sainted and yet can perform miracles, greater things than the miracles performed by the saints of the altars, because these spirits that aren't sainted go on wandering through the world, they don't disappear, they live among us, they can give us advice.

—JOSÉ DONOSO, *THE OBSCENE BIRD OF NIGHT*

Verse 1

PETA PONCE WAS born a stranger in her body. Her head was too big for her stocky torso. Her arms were uneven, as if the hunchback she carried was where the rest of her right arm had been left behind. She was a black-as-tar woman who as a child had known nothing but sadness. Her parents feared that their future children would be born like her, too, and so they hated their firstborn. In the village of Cabo Rojo, like its red salt mines, Peta Ponce was put to work. She dusted, swept, cut, iron, cooked, folded, and served, and not once did she hold on to bitterness.

One day the doctors arrived in Cabo Rojo, the way they were showing up in many villages, with their black bags and government-issued vans. These doctors were hired, sent by the government not to educate, or to heal, but to see which of the women in that particular village were unfit, feeble-minded, or "promiscuous" in their eyes. When they caught sight of Peta Ponce, Salvador told me, they saw not a young girl but a thing that they were going to make sure would be the last of its kind. The doctors assured Peta Ponce's parents that this was beneficial for her "appendix," which needed to be removed, but in fact her appendix was healthy. They gave the parents and Peta Ponce no information, no options, and no choice. Her parents accepted what the doctors were saying as if it came from the mouth of God. All of the people in Cabo Rojo believed these doctors. They did not know that these doctors often made medical records appear as if the sterilization were necessary for the health of the young girls. The peasant population of Cabo Rojo did not understand, Salvador told me, that for the United States, Puerto Rico was a source of cheap labor, high profit, and tax-free business and a testing area for population control. Even the Pill was first tested there. Everyone was in on it. Everyone was on the take. The doctors were paid by the Puerto Rican government, which in turn was reimbursed by the United States. The church got its hush money, and the colonization of wombs went into effect for decades.

Salvador told me that many were in the dark. These doctors arrived in a village of farmers, of peasants, of poor folks and cured some people while sterilizing women. And no one questioned anything. But everyone felt a sad silence once the doctors were gone.

It was then, Salvador told me, when Peta Ponce realized that in order to fight this she would have to learn how to talk with the dead.

Peta Ponce left Cabo Rojo. She wandered from village to village, sleeping in churches, beauty salons, markets, huts, riverbeds, fields, anyplace where that particular town's *espiritistas, santeros,* eccentrics, and mystics were willing to see her, talk to her, share what they knew about the dead. She wandered all over the island picking up bits and pieces of folklore, superstition, *chisme,* every bit of our Taíno roots, African roots, Catholic mysticism, from *espiritismo* to Mesa Blanca, to Palo Monte, to Regla Lukumi. Peta Ponce absorbed it all. Village mystic elders never failed to see a light following her.

One night, in Guayama, the village of Los Brujos, Peta Ponce, in her sweaty old clothes that reeked of rice and rum, was taken to the riverbanks. In those violent shallow waters Peta Ponce was baptized an *espiritista* by older mystics to whom, Salvador said, the spirits had whispered that this young woman had been born with a gift to make people see a "Thou" where they once saw an "it." Peta Ponce knew all the palm trees, the plants, the hills, the swamps, the *coquís,* the cemeteries, the heat, the rivers, the ravines, the rocks, the iguanas, the snakes and pastures of dirt, the cats who roamed El Morro at night, the entire island spoke to her in this language where reality and imagination, waking and dreaming, could switch places. And somehow Peta Ponce had always known these things, like children who knew their prayers but could not remember from whom they had learned them.

One night, by a lonely riverbank, Sal told me, during a baptismal ceremony a scream was heard. It started out low and slow and it seemed to bubble right out of the mud, higher and angrier. It was a hateful scream that formed words that were not human. They were shrieks that held meaning only in some other realm. The screaming woman was being held down tightly by three other women who grappled with her in the mud. The three *espiritistas* could not calm the screaming woman. Until Peta Ponce arrived. She ordered the three women to let the screaming woman go. When the muddied woman looked up at Peta Ponce, she quieted down, as if Peta Ponce were the only person who could understand her language. The muddied woman's eyes began to focus little by little, as if she were returning from a great distance and discovering the world all over again. Trembling, the woman clutched Peta Ponce's ragged gown and begged her not to let her die again. And, Salvador said, Peta Ponce whispered to the woman that with the help of the dead she would change the definitions, the meanings, of her sorrows.

Like those doctors before, Peta Ponce went from village to village. Her monstrous presence was frightening to the men, but the women would seek her like iron fillings to a magnet. Women who had prayed to all the gods their mothers had known. Women who had prayed to all the saints they had inherited from their grandmothers. Women who had prayed all their lives but had received no peace, these women sought Peta Ponce. She could capture their feelings of regret, of shame, of being coerced, of abuse, and turn the definitions of these terrible emotions into something else. She could fold, twist, and turn experiences around so far back that what had happened was seen in a completely different light. The words that described these terrible emotions held new definitions. It was the spirits who lent her the power to interweave, to curl, twirl, and ripple emotions so that the soul could find its way back to happiness.

To Peta Ponce, there existed an invisible foundation. It was this unseen plane that held up the material one. The material world was not just ours; we shared it with the dead. The dead were all around us, leaping from material to spiritual. Malice was not what the spirits were after, but rather finding a balance in having to share the material world with the living. They existed in a constant fluidity of sadness for no longer being flesh and blood and also of gratitude for still existing in some other state. Peta Ponce believed that there existed only one plane where the dead could never go. And that was where God lived. And that not even the dead had seen God's face, for God did not dwell with the dead. The dead stayed here on earth and wandered the planet, living among us. The dead were here to guide us, to help us understand that everything is just a matter of turns. When it's your turn to leave the material world, the dead would be there to help you in this new phase of life. Because just as there were people waiting for you when you were born, Peta Ponce preached, there would be people waiting for you when you passed.

Much later, Peta Ponce founded a school, a little house of her own, La Casa de Ejercicios Espirituales de la Encarnación. And broken women came, some stayed, some left, but their stories were all the same. Women who had been lied to, coerced, misinformed, or forced into *la operación*. Women who were forced to lose children in order to work, or women who were abused, beaten in any way, they all needed Peta Ponce to reverse the definitions of their sadness.

Peta Ponce's name quickly made its way to the mainland. *La operación* was happening there, too, from the South Bronx, the Lower East Side, Bushwick, Spanish Harlem,

Chicago, Philadelphia, New Jersey, Los Angeles, Hartford, Boston: everywhere there was a woman peddling at a sweatshop, a factory, a cash register, or while mopping some office, it was happening. The bosses wanted the women making them money, not making children. As a whole, the United States did not want Puerto Rican women reproducing. It was not birth control but population control. The choice was left not to the women but to the state. Poor childbearing women were the culprits of poverty. The more children they birthed, the more poverty would grow, the more easily vulnerable Puerto Rico would be to communist ideals.

When Sal told me all this, I was in awe and full of fear in meeting Peta Ponce.

PETA PONCE ARRIVED at Taína's house dressed all in white. Her hair was tightly tucked inside a bandanna, where a carnation stuck out like a white ear. She carried her short, uneven body hard. Her steps were heavy, as if she wanted to break the floors underneath her. She combed Taína's apartment, smelling every corner like a new puppy. Peta Ponce dug her fingernails over the walls, too, as if she needed to leave scratches behind. Her appearance and actions did scare me, as I felt relieved that she had finally arrived.

The kitchen table was covered with a white mantle, white flowers, and white candles. Puerto Rican plates were spread out, some had been eaten from, as Doña Flores had granted the *espiritista* and Taína a feast, while some plates lay untouched for the spirits. In the living room Taína sat scared. She was wearing a long, beautiful white dress. Her hair was loose, neatly draping down her shoulders. Newly done eyelashes framed her hazel eyes, and her nervous lips were a soft red. Taína's stomach was a globe. It was only a matter of days before she'd give birth. I had never seen Taína look this beautiful and so familiar. When Taína saw that I was there, she exhaled and smiled slightly but did not move. Taína was clearly afraid of Peta Ponce, because she didn't utter a single curse.

I had brought the money with me and was about to sit on the floor next to Sal.

"Afuera, Juan Bobo," Doña Flores said in Spanish, and held out a hand for the money.

"Taína wants me here," I said in Spanish, as it was the language that we all mostly spoke in the entire night.

Salvador nodded to his sister that it was okay.

"No"—Doña Flores shook her head—"this is about family. And Juan Bobo is not family."

I turned to the *espiritista* for help.

"Familia, no más," Peta Ponce said.

Taína's mouth opened in panic. She leaned up a bit as if she were going to protest my leaving. But I knew Taína was not going to go against her mother's wishes.

"Then I'm taking the money with me," I said.

"No, you already promised to give it to me so I can pay the *espiritista*," Doña Flores said.

"Inelda, this ain't right," Salvador said. I knew how highly she held his words, so I thought I would be able to stay.

"He disturbs the spirits, they do not know who he is," she said to her brother, whom she took as a saint. "What happened in this house only the spirits know, and he is not part of this house."

Salvador nodded in agreement. He then bowed to Peta Ponce.

I also bowed to the small woman who could fold time, twist definitions, change the meaning of feelings, and talk to the dead.

"Juan Bobo," Doña Flores said kindly, "give me the money. You can see Ta-te after we learn the truth."

"No," I said. "Then I'll go, but I'm leaving with the money." I looked at Taína. "I will see you again, okay?" Taína slightly nodded her head because she was scared. And it was there, when she slightly nodded at me, that I knew she might love me, too, regardless of all her bossy insults.

Doña Flores began to curse.

"¡Malcriado, puñeta!" she spat. "Give me the money. You promised."

I headed for the door and heard the *espiritista* ask Sal if anyone else had money. When he said no, the *espiritista* told me to wait.

"¿Tu nombre, mijo?" Peta Ponce asked.

"Julio," I said, "not Juan Bobo. My name is Julio." And then Peta Ponce began to sniff the air around me, the spaces around me, and began to touch all my clothes and sniff them, too, she touched me everywhere like some obscene bird of night.

"De rodillas," she ordered. I knelt and she took my head in her hands and brought my face toward her heavy breasts and began to pray.

"Santa Marta, recurro a la ayuda y protección; como prueba de mi afecto quemare esta vela cada martes; intercede por mi familia, y protége a este extraño." And then like something had been told to her, she pushed my body away and I fell on the floor in front of her.

"Los espíritus ya saben quién es este muchacho," Peta Ponce said, and then looked down at me. *"Tu madre, yo sentí a tu madre,"* she said. I stayed on the floor, afraid of this woman who through me had felt my mother.

But she had not come for my mother or me, or Sal, or Doña Flores; she had made the trek all the way from Cabo Rojo for Taína.

Doña Flores had paid Peta Ponce's plane fare, but she had not paid the *espiritista* for the séance.

"El derecho, pa' lo' espíritus," Peta Ponce demanded. I got up from the floor and dug into my pocket. I held the wad of hundreds toward Peta Ponce. Disgusted, she slapped my hand away.

"Inelda." The *espiritista* pointed at Doña Flores. *"El derecho me lo da Inelda."*

I didn't see a difference, but I did as told. I gave the wad to Doña Flores and she in turn gave it to the *espiritista*. Peta Ponce didn't count it, she simply split the wad of hundreds in half and stuffed her bra left and right, as if creating a balance in her body.

She ordered Doña Flores to fill a bowl with water mixed with *agua maravilla* and to light a white candle and place both items on the table in the living room, where she was going to summon the spirits who lived in Taína's house.

Those spirits who were present when Taína became pregnant. It would be these spirits who would tell her how it had happened.

Peta Ponce went over to where Taína sat on the couch. Peta Ponce helped Taína's pregnant body stand back on its feet. Peta Ponce smiled lovingly and whispered to Taína in the kindest of voices not to be afraid.

She told Taína that spirits live with us, *mi bella*. They hover over our sleeping bodies, *¿tú sabes?* She then took Taína's hand as if Taína were a toddler, and the two women went inside Taína's bedroom and the *espiritista* closed the door.

I heard murmurs, whispers, a soft voice ordering Taína to show her all her clothes, jewelry, medicine, tampons. That she needed to make contact with these things because spirits leave behind traces of themselves. That spirits touch our things, wear our clothes, and sniff our wastes when we are not present. They warm their hands over our sleeping bodies like they are campfires to recall what it felt like to be flesh and blood. And that the opposite is true, it is we who appear transparent and opaque to the spirits and sometimes they need *us* to guide *them*.

When Taína and Peta Ponce came back out, Taína was wearing the same sleeping gown I had seen her in. It must have been the gown from the night she found out she was pregnant. Holding Taína's hand, the *espiritista* took her all around the apartment. Peta Ponce sniffed every corner, all the while reciting quick, short prayers as she licked her fingertips after touching walls and floors.

When she stopped praying, Peta Ponce turned off the

lights. Only the candles lit the house. She ordered for all to be still. She pulled out the white carnation that was trapped at the side of her face by the white bandanna and dipped it in the bowl full of water. She sprinkled each of us with the carnation and said, *"Como el dia que nacimos, fue una mujer que no' conectó a Dios."* Like the day we were born, it was a woman who connected us to God.

Doña Flores sat on the couch. Salvador sat next to her. I was sitting on the floor. The *espiritista* sat Taína on a chair and stood behind her. The short, stocky woman was not towering over Taína, but she was higher than a sitting Taína.

The bowl of water was not far away from Peta Ponce. She circled her finger around the bowl, flicked her index finger on the glass, making the sound of a bell, as if signifying to the universe that this *misa* was about to begin.

The *espiritista* did nothing but stand behind a seated Taína. Nothing was happening. All Peta Ponce did was stare ahead.

There was silence for what seemed like forever.

Then.

Peta Ponce began to moan, a drone moan like a steady engine.

Peta Ponce closed her eyes.

Her fingers began to move as they made their way toward Taína's hair. She brushed Taína's hair slowly at first, but soon her fingers began to pick up speed, brushing faster and faster like she was shampooing Taína's hair. Then she left Taína's hair alone and now began to rub her hands together really quickly, as if she were building a fire. The movements picked up more speed, and she stomped her heavy, short feet to a steady rhythm and began clapping her hands all around. Her musical movements increased, her moaning got louder and louder as she entered the unrecognizable language of the spirit world.

"Who was here, that night, that night? That day?" she yelled in Spanish to the walls. The same walls that Doña Flores spoke to. "Who was there, that day? That night?" she implored, and then her body shook. Peta Ponce began rubbing Taína's arms up and down, and then she started clapping, asking the spirits who was there. Then, with a graceful and quick motion, she picked up the lit white candle lying on the table, and as if picking up fire itself, she flicked the flames into the bowl of water and drowned the candle's fire and screamed.

Taína's eyes were drowsy, like she was about to fall asleep. Her head dropped. All I could see was hair covering her face. She sat motionless while Peta Ponce made all this noise and recited prayers in some language I did not know.

Then the *espiritista* stopped like she had been kicked in the throat.

She stood straight up behind a sleeping Taína. She outstretched her arms and began to gracefully wave them up and down like they were wings, and she began to talk in English.

"I was lying in my bed at night," the *espiritista,* eyes closed, softly said, "when the doves arrived." It was a young girl's voice, though it was Peta Ponce who was talking. "I was lying down when two doves flew in through my window. Both were white, pure, and beautiful." When the *espiritista* opened her eyes, her whole demeanor had changed.

She heaved her breasts as if she were in awe of a boy. Her hunchback fluttered as if it were flirting, slowly, gracefully.

"They flew in through my window. They kept leaping, flying around my bedroom. Sometimes they would crash in midair like they were kissing. One was whiter than the other. Both doves landed on my pink rug, the one Mami had bought me at the ninety-nine-cent store." And Doña Flores silently nodded her head in agreement that this was so. "Two pretty birds staring at each other." The *espiritista* batted her eyes as if she were flirting. "Both doves looked at me and took a step forward. They faced each other and then at me and back at each other again. I don't know when, but their wings began to grow. Slowly and muscular like tree trunks their wings became huge and so did the rest of their bodies. Their eyes began to shine a white light that made them transparent like ghosts." The *espiritista* was gracefully waving her arms like she had done before, like a seagull flying in the heavens. She waved her arms and continued to sound like a schoolgirl. "They began to make those sounds that pigeons make like popcorn or chickens but not exactly like popcorn or chickens. They began to speak like that to each other and the sounds became angrier. They began to hit each other. But not with their hands. Not their arms. Not their feet or their heads or teeth, which they did have. They began to hit each other with their enormous wings and they knocked my schoolbooks down and almost broke the mirror that hangs by my closet."

Doña Flores couldn't stand it anymore and she blurted out, "Where was I when this was happening? Where was I?" In anger, the *espiritista*'s head quickly jerked toward Doña

Flores and with the voice of Peta Ponce, it said, "Asleep on the couch. I will leave if you talk again."

And I got cold.

I was not going to interrupt about a revolution in Taína's body or anything because this had scared me.

Then back to speaking in a schoolgirl's voice, Peta Ponce continued.

"The birds beat each other with their wings in quick slaps. I thought it was a dance, but it wasn't and I became afraid. The doves were male and I closed my legs and crossed my hands like this." And the *espiritista* covered her crotch. And still with the voice of a young girl, she spoke in fear and panic. "I was trembling. I tried to scream, but nothing came out. I tried to scream. The two doves were not doves but angels. The angels were fighting. All I could do was keep my hands where I had them. I was sure that one of the angels was going to hurt the other. The whiter one hit the less white angel and it fell to the rug. With his wings the whiter angel kept hitting the one on the floor as he lay on top of my rug. Then the whiter angel leaped up and flew around my room real fast to pick up speed. He then swooped down and pounced on the helpless angel that was lying on the rug. He had talons. The angel had talons." The *espiritista* got on her knees and, while still behind a seated and sleeping Taína, embraced her. She wrapped her short arms around Taína as if she were her mother. Peta Ponce began to cry as the spirits continued to lend her the power to fold time. "The whiter angel was now beating the darker one with his talons nonstop. At first the darker one tried to avoid getting stepped on or kicked. He tried to block the blows with his wings as best he could, but little by little he began to give up till he stopped and just lay there like a dead bird and took all the blows."

Salvador moved closer to the edge of the couch and Doña Flores took in a huge gulp. I didn't know what to make of any of this.

"The dark angel began to cry like a baby and I saw that his wing had been broken. When I opened my eyes the dark angel looked at me for only a second, but I didn't really look back at him and he must have gone out my window because I did not see him again. I had had the lights on all this time, but my room was dark. And soon the white angel was hovering above me. I could see his enormous wings almost not fitting in my room. I felt his shadow above me, covering me. He flew down, nearer to my bed where I had not moved. I closed my eyes and then opened them again to make sure it was the whiter angel. I closed my legs even tighter. I opened my eyes just a little. I saw he had blue eyes. They were gentle. I could hear the angel tell me to lay still. The white angel said, 'Shhh,' and I don't know why he was telling me to 'Shhh' because I had been quiet all this time. Not using his hands, or his arms, or his mouth, only the tip of his wings, he began to unlock my hands where I had them. At first I did not want to move my hands but leave them where I had them, covering me. But when he touched me with the tip of his wing, his feathers felt like a wind. A gentle wind."

Still embracing Taína, the *espiritista* began to whistle as if a fresh current had entered through the closed window. Her whistling swirled around the living room.

"What did the angel do?" Doña Flores interrupted again. But the spirit did not do as it had said. But she spoke back.

"He did what he had been sent out to do." The *espiritista*'s voice was still that of a young girl's. "What he had been sent to do."

"Did the angel take off his pants?" Doña Flores asked. The *espiritista* laughed.

"Angels don't wear pants," she said, still trancelike and embracing Taína, who sat there motionless and asleep.

"He only used his wings?" Doña Flores asked.

"No. No wings." Still in the same schoolgirl voice. "He didn't use anything. He hovered over me and things began to move. My room was spinning. And then it stopped like a fan dying. I wanted to sleep."

"No pain?" Doña Flores asked.

"No." The *espiritista*'s eyes were still closed.

"Blood, was there blood?" Doña Flores repeated.

"I felt water come out of me. And the white angel brushed a feather from his wing over it and the water was gone. Then he flew out my window. I got up from my bed to look out the window to see him flying. What I saw was the dove staring up at me, perched on the mailbox across the street." And the *espiritista*'s eyes suddenly opened. "He was telling me his name, Usmaíl."

There was silence for a second and then half a second.

"Padre nuestro que estás en los cielos, santificado sea tu nombre, que se haga tu voluntad en los cielos como en la tierra." Peta Ponce began to pray. She was coming back to us, to the material world that we shared with the dead. She was exhausted.

Peta Ponce got up and went to where the bowl of water was and began sprinkling water all around the living room. *"Limpieza, limpieza, limpieza."*

Taína slowly awoke and said she had not dreamed. That she had just slept. Deeply. Peta Ponce began to clue Taína in on what the spirit who had been present when she became pregnant had just told us.

"Why would God send two angels? Why two?" Taína asked Peta Ponce, who always smiled warmly at her.

"Dios no mandó dos ángeles," she explained to Taína with a kindness found only in grandmothers, *"Dios mandó sólo uno."*

"Then who sent the other freaking angel?"

"Tú sabe' quien, mija, el Negro. El Malo," Peta Ponce said with compassionate eyes. She knelt down and began to gently rub Taína's feet. Like I had.

Taína was satisfied. I could almost hear her happy heart pounding as she accepted this. Taína embraced the *espiritista* for having set her free. She held Peta Ponce like she wanted to take the air out of the small woman because her sorrows and uncertainty were now gone or had been changed.

Doña Flores laughed. Her joy was immense. She could not stop and literally danced to the closet where Taína had taken me before. She opened it like she was opening French doors or a vault that held treasures. Her massive library of Taína's baby instruments came crashing down. They spilled all over the floor like Cheerios. Her face was aglow. But it was not Taína's baby instruments she was after. She got a chair and brought down those old records, the 45s, the 33⅓

LPs, those brittle 78s, like someone who hadn't eaten in days and now, in front of a buffet, didn't know what to choose. Sal went over to help. Doña Flores smiled my way. I knew she wanted money for a stereo system.

Taína then loudly said that she needed to pee. She was a bit flushed and, with very little trouble, picked up her pregnant body from the chair she had been sitting on. She gave me this smile, this shy smile, as she waddled her stomach toward the kitchen. There she drank water, picked up a leftover chicken leg, and walked to the bathroom, did not close the door, sat on the bowl, peed, and ate.

Verse 2

I SAID TO Salvador that I didn't believe it.

I respected Peta Ponce, but she or that spirit was wrong. I hadn't had a chance to talk to Taína because as soon as the *misa* ended, Doña Flores, happy as a sunflower, ushered me and Salvador out because she wanted to be alone with Peta Ponce. I said to Sal that we had been to outer space. We had a good idea of what was there. But we had never been to inner space where atoms live. We'd never sent astronauts or probes there so we didn't know what existed between all that empty space. That was where Usmaíl was conceived, in Taína's inner heavens. I told Sal that I had read that there were patterns in everything. Even in chaos, things happened that were tied together by some order. Maybe in Taína's body this order or pattern changed. Something went wrong or maybe it went right. The laws of her DNA got crossed or were never meant to be followed.

Salvador said that this would mean that atoms were sentient, atoms were alive and could think. He said this was not so. I said to Sal that it was a possibility, I didn't know. How did we know if anything could think? I said to Sal, a rock or a fish or a lobster or a pencil, there were atoms inside those things, too, like there were atoms in us. Like the atoms in Taína's body. All it took was just one, one of them to rebel. But in his eyes I saw he didn't want to talk about this. It wasn't important to him. Like everyone else, after what Peta Ponce had discovered, the case was closed.

Before leaving me on the street that night, Salvador said, "Listen, *papo,* if Taína believes in two angels arriving at night fighting to be Usmaíl's father, it's fine." And he placed a bony hand on my shoulder. "If you believe that a revolution began inside Taína's body, inside, way inside, where atoms live, that is okay, too, *papo*. The world is big enough for everything," he said, and right before his long legs took him away, he looked at me kindly. "You know, *papo,* you are my only friend. I never had that many friends. In all my life I never had that many. Maybe none. Thank you, you know, for everything, *papo*."

I didn't go straight home that night. I took the elevator to the roof of the building. I looked at the Manhattan skyline and wondered if anything I had just heard and saw made sense.

And then I saw something.

I was no longer on the roof.

I was walking around Central Park's north side. There was ozone in the city air. The pond was clean. Kids were fishing by the Charles A. Dana Discovery Center. On the benches and on the grass, there were people of many colors and countries, Africans and African Americans as well as

Latinos from all over the Americas, all taking in the sun. And I saw things.

I saw a crystal city.

Skyscrapers built out of glass.

A city of light, color, and endless possibilities. This city had a green rectangular park running down its middle, dividing its west from its east. It had a hole in the ground where everyday people of all colors, income brackets, genders, and sexual preferences traveled. It had four satellites that circled it or completed it into a city of one of five. And then I saw us, all three of us. Usmaíl was no longer inside Taína's body. Taína was stretched out, sleeping on a blanket in a green field in that park. Her hair spilled all around me, her figure inviting, her arms and legs exposed, thin and lovely as if she were nobody's mother. Across from us, a teenage Usmaíl was ice-skating, though it was summer, and no one skates on the Harlem Meer even when it freezes in the winter. Taína continued sleeping. I got up. I saw how gracefully and elegantly Usmaíl skated. Then Usmaíl glided over to me. "The important thing," Usmaíl said, "is not how I got here. The important thing is that I'm here now. You gonna take care of me or what?"

BECAUSE I HAD grown tired of being bullied by Mario and because there was no way I was going to pay him every month, no way, I had done something I was not proud of. There was no going back. Like Sal, all I could do was try to rewrite something good from what I could not change. To get back at Mario, I had signed up using his name and address for a year's subscription to a gay porn magazine called *Blue Boy*. I had added to the cart two vibrators, a whip, and a leather mask. I knew that when Mario's father got those things in the mail, he was going to throw a fit. I wanted Mario to feel that humiliation. I wanted him to feel that fear and discomfort. I wanted his father to beat him up like Mario had beaten me up. I didn't expect, though, that his father was going to send him to the hospital.

BD and I were outside Metropolitan Hospital.

"I ain't going in," BD said.

"We should."

"Why? This is what we wanted. Think about him picking on us at lunchtime, calling us wetbacks."

"We have to say something to him."

"He took my arm."

"You got it back."

"He wanted a cut from our work."

"So? We were as much hustlers as he was trying to hustle us."

"So what nothing."

"Come on, BD. We owe Mario at least to say sorry." Mario was turning twenty-one, and the system was either going to pass him so he could graduate with a high school diploma or drop him altogether because he was a super-duper super-senior. Either way, we would not have to deal with him at school anymore, and yet I felt bad.

"This was your idea. Not mine. You're the one with bright ideas. I'm staying right here." He crossed his arms, sat on a bench, and was not going to be moved. "Staying right here." He dug out his Jolly Ranchers.

I opened Metropolitan Hospital's door. The air conditioner on full blast told me that the school year was almost over. Taína's due date was ahead.

"Are you family? In order to visit, you must be family," the woman at the visiting hours desk said.

"Yes. I'm family," I said.

"You don't look Italian."

"He's my half cousin." Here I was going to see the neighborhood racist bully and saying he had my blood.

She scoped me for only a second, then shrugged like it was not her problem.

"The room number is written right here." The receptionist pointed. I took the big blue plastic card with the word VISITOR in big, black, bold letters and rode up the elevator. I took out the comic books I had hidden inside my pants because I was embarrassed to tell BD that I had bought Mario comics. I had bought the ones he was always reading, Sandman series, Dark Knight, and X-Men. When I stepped off the elevator, I didn't go in Mario's room. I stayed outside and peered through the slightly opened door. Mario looked like a guy who just wanted to be left alone. I think he knew what they were saying about him back in school. About a rumor that I had started. That big, bad Mario De Puma was gay, and when his father found out, he sent him to the hospital. All the kids were laughing behind his back.

Mario was propped up with pillows behind his back. His jaw was wired up. His arm was in a cast, though both his legs were fine. I slowly walked in, and in discomfort and pain Mario turned his head.

"Fuck . . . you . . . want?" Clenched jaw sounding like Clint Eastwood.

"Nothing." I forced a smile.

"Cops . . . got . . . you?"

"Almost but not yet."

"Your . . . scam . . . about?"

"Doesn't matter. It's over."

"Too . . . bad," he said, and hurt something because he took a quick breath and then he said to me, "Sorry." I saw steel wires in his mouth, rubber bands, too.

"For what, man?"

"Ruining . . . your . . . thing."

"It's cool," I said, and he looked at me, wanting to know why I was there. But I wasn't going to tell him, no way. I was there because it was my personal way of apologizing. I was no different from him. I had exploited a fear of something that is really natural. Something that shouldn't matter. But in Spanish Harlem it did, and I knew it sure as hell mattered to Mario's father. I knew that boys could be brutal, and this brutality wasn't always displayed by physical violence. I had hurt Mario, and it was just as brutal as if I had stabbed him.

"School . . . what are . . . they . . . saying . . . about me? In . . . ?" Through gritted teeth, he got all that out.

"That you're a jerk."

"That's . . . it?"

"Yes," I lied.

"Sure?"

"Yes, and that you deserved it for being a jerk."

And I think he was happy with this.

"Okay . . . good."

"You know, Mario," I said, "we are just two kids stuck in this place with no money. We don't know any better. You know, we are just trying."

I left him the comics by his bed. With more discomfort and pain, he twisted his head.

"Old issues . . . read already." Though I knew he had not read those because the man at the comic store told me they had just come out that day. Still, I didn't say anything.

"See you in school," I said, and he barely nodded back. And just as I was about to turn toward the door, he grunted.

"Wait . . . Taína . . ." He took a deep breath because whatever he was going to say was a lot and it was going to hurt him. "If you see . . . her . . . say . . . I . . . want . . . to . . . talk to her."

No way was I going to say this to Taína.

"Sure," I said.

"Okay." He was spent. The painkillers were bombarding his body with sleep. I took one last look at the guy and realized that Mario had all the tools and makings of a stand-up guy, if he could only learn how to make those tools work and pull himself together.

Verse 3

I SHOULD HAVE known something was wrong when I entered and there was no music in our house. My mother was waiting, arms crossed like Mussolini. "All those books on pregnancy . . ." Mom shook her head. "You think I'm stupid. A woman knows." She had gone into my room and searched my stuff. *"Una mujer sabe."* She lifted her hand as if to strike me but didn't. "Why would you have books on pregnancy?" She huffed and puffed. "I know you are still going down there." Her lips were tight, like a child who doesn't want to open them for the dentist. "Those women who live on the second floor"—she was doing her best to keep her anger in check—"any criminal could have come through that window. I'm losing a day's work. *Pero esto se acaba hoy, señorito."* Not seeing my father get up from all this shouting told me he had agreed to this.

On the Metro-North up to Ossining, Mom repeated, "I'm doing this for you. *Que el Señor me ayude.* I'm doing this for you." I didn't need to see that man. I had my truth on how Taína had gotten pregnant. Peta Ponce had another meaning, another definition. Taína had chosen to believe that. But none of this mattered anymore. Once, I had gone to see this man myself to look for answers and come away empty-handed, but now there were no more questions to be answered. But Mom wouldn't understand. Mom had planned this because that man's mother was waiting for us by the shuttle that would take us to the prison's compound.

After the ride, we entered the prison's visiting hall, and I was hit by all this white noise. Inmates and their families murmuring, coughing, laughing, yelling, kissing, babies crying. Soon, an unshackled and uncuffed Orlando Castillo walked into the hall, led by a guard. He could have easily passed for a white man. He had blond hair and seagull-pale blue eyes. He was the whitest of Puerto Ricans I had ever seen. We were seated next to his mother and he glanced at Mom and me for only a second before slowly sitting down in front of us. With only a table and glass in the middle separating us. There was no need for phones; the glass was not that high and it had holes in it. The man smiled at his mother and she smiled back at him. He placed his hand on the glass and she did, too. I did not see any violence in his face, only happiness that his mother had come to visit him. I looked at Mom at my side to maybe tell her that we should leave them alone, we could question him a little later. But my mother's eyes were lost on another prisoner sitting about two families away from us. As if I did not exist, as if she had forgotten why she had dragged me all the way here, she got up and slowly walked the few steps, where sat an irritated white woman visiting her jailed husband across the table.

"Bobby?" Mom whispered to herself. *"¿Ese eres tú?"* she said louder. The guy took his gaze off his wife and looked up at Mom, squinting as if the sun were in his face.

"Oh, shit. *Mami,*" he said out loud among all that white noise. My mother forced an embarrassed short smile. "*Mami,* shit, wha' you doing here?" he said, even more embarrassed than my mother. Still sitting, his wife scoped my mother, nodded angrily, and sucked in some teeth. They had never met before but had always known about each other. "This is my wife, Angel." From across the glass he pointed at a pretty, short, white woman sitting in front of him. She was dressed in jeans and a coffee-stained blouse. Her hair was in a bun held by like a hundred bobby pins. She was wearing these flat-topped platform shoes to make her look taller. My mother guiltily held out her hand.

"Why don't you"—the wife ignored my mother's hand—"get him his chicken-shit sandwich and Coke?" And not taking her eyes off him, she gave the guard a half-full paper bag for inspection. The guard looked in it and then placed it next to her husband, who sat across the table.

"Yeah, yeah, you just tell Junito to come see me," he yelled as his wife began walking away. "This is bullshit. I'm still his father, *coño,* no matter how old he is now." His wife gave him the finger and then continued to walk away. He then smiled at my mother as if none of this had happened. My mother politely and full of embarrassment smiled back, but she did not take the now empty seat in front him. She stayed standing, and when he stood up so as to be eye to eye with my mother, a guard yelled, "Sit the fuck down." He sat down, and my mother's nose started to run.

"Do you want a chicken sandwich and Coke, Bobby? I'll get it," Mom said nicely, still standing.

"*De verdad*?" he said. "That would be great, you know the food in here is for *pericos*. You, Mami, you don't look anything like I thought you would by now."

"De verdad?" Mom said. "I think you look good, still looking good." But I knew she didn't mean it. His face was a pothole of craters, and whatever it was that he had done to finally land him in prison was written in his features.

"Yeah, you know I'm still a *pollo*. But I thought you'd be better-looking after all these years." And from Mom's expression, I think she was holding on to some hope that a tiny bit of what she had once fallen for was still there. "That's your son?" he said, and Mom just nodded. I nodded back at him. "Wha's your name?"

"I'll get you a sandwich," I said, not telling him.

"Chevere," he said happily. "And a Coke. Diet, okay? And could you get me coffee, put lots of sugar in it, okay, and get me some cookies, chips, pretzels, and a Snickers." He quickly licked his lips. "Oh, and an egg-salad sandwich for later, pretzels, two bags, can you do that?"

I did as Mom did by only nodding. I walked to the back of the visiting hall. There were six vending machines lined up side by side like six extra guards. One sold cookies, one sold coffee, one sold sandwiches, one sodas, the others chips and chocolate bars. I took out some bills I had, and as I slid the dollars in each machine, on the vending glass I caught glimpses of what was happening behind me. My mother was still standing, and Bobby *"el Pollo con la Voz"* Arroyo was sitting and talking really fast, his hands moving rapidly as if he were afraid my mother would walk away before he was done. Once in a while my mom would switch her weight, but she did not say much, I'm sure. I could tell she was only listening, even among all that noise, I knew that she was not the one talking. There were plastic bags from a dispenser, and I placed all the stuff he had asked for. I then rejoined him and Mom, and he kept laughing and smiling and saying, "Believe me, *mami, mamita, la salsera,* my love. You have to believe me. *Lo juro.* On the life of my children, *lo juro.*"

On her face I didn't see any love for him, only politeness and maybe some terrible memories that were rolling past Mom. She hadn't said a word and had stayed standing, continually staring at her past. When I motioned to the guard to come take the items from me for inspection, my mother said, "Let's go."

"But what about . . . ?" I said, pointing two seats down to where that man was lovingly talking to his mother. *" 'Tá bien. 'Tá todo bien,"* she said, and then looked at Bobby, who was happy when the guard brought him over more stuff. "You know, Bobby, I forgive you," Mom said, getting ready to leave.

"You forgive me?" he said, laughing. "*Coño,* shit. You forgive me? I brought excitement to your boring fucking life and you forgive me? *Pa' carajo.*"

"You mistreated me. Things I won't repeat, but I forgive you, Bobby," she said.

"*Mierda,* I made your life special and you say you forgive me, shit. That's fucked up, you know. I should be the one forgiving you! You were so boring before you met me, and you say you want to forgive me?"

Mom then really looked into his eyes, held them for a long time, before saying, *"Que Dios te cuide."*

"No, 'pera, mami, wait, *nena, 'pera,"* he said desperately when Mom cleared her runny nose and turned her back on him. "Wait, I'm sorry, I'm sorry. You know everyone was crazy back then. Crazy. *Todo el mundo.* You know, *mami*?"

Mom continued walking and I followed her. His desperation grew. "Listen, can you visit again?" we both heard him say loudly. "Just bring me stuff. Toothpaste, some clothes? Okay? *¿Mami? . . . ¿Mami?"* he yelled. "Just some stuff, okay? . . . Okay?" When he knew she was not coming back, his voice sailed. "See how you treat me? See how you treat me? Fuck you."

ON THE WAY back my mother said nothing. She stared ahead and once in a while would look my way but never say anything. I left her alone and rode the long ride back to the Metro-North Spanish Harlem stop on 125th Street and Park.

When we arrived home my father was cooking. In Spanish he asked, "How did it go?" But my mother didn't answer and went straight to the bedroom and closed the door. My father followed her and knocked. Was everything all right? he asked. I thought she was going to yell to leave her alone.

"I'm fine," she said nicely through the closed door. "I'm fine."

My father looked at me, asking what happened. I repeated that she was fine. He asked again what had happened. I said nothing. He squeezed my shoulder, letting me know he did not believe me, but just then he heard one of his pots overflowing and he ran back to the kitchen.

The last dog I was to take back was still running around. I fed him, but he didn't want to eat because my father must have fed him already. I went to my room and looked through some of my books. I could not read and put the books aside. I thought about Peta Ponce, about the two doves becoming angels and fighting to be Usmaíl's father. I thought, Why should I believe only in one thing? The inner heavens were so large that there was enough room to believe in everything. Peta Ponce folded time in order to change definitions and meanings so scarred women could find peace. I was at peace, too, because the revolution had occurred. And the only one who needed this definition was me.

I heard a knock. I thought it was my father because Mom just entered. But it was her. She was not crying or anything and she was wearing the earrings I had bought her. Her face was gentle and polite, expressions she showed only in public. She asked for permission to sit on my bed. I laughed a little and told her, "Yeah, you bought it."

"I never meant when I said *pa'* Lincoln," she said nicely. "I would never leave you at that hospital." This made me happy because I had always believed that she might. "But if I did leave you, I'd visit you every day." She knew herself well, because when Mom is angry she is capable of anything. God help you if you ever doubt a Puerto Rican woman.

"Ma," I said, but she didn't let me say anything after that. She asked me if I missed not having any brothers and sisters. I didn't answer because she wanted to tell me things she had never told and would never tell me again.

"You like that girl. *Una madre sabe.*"

"Yeah," I said. "She's something like you, I think?"

"Kids are like their parents, and if Taína is like her mother, she's . . ."

"Talented? Taína is talented. Like her mother, she can sing," I said.

"Fine. But that's not what I meant." Mom's nose began to run again. "I know Inelda. She's crazy."

"We are all crazy, Ma. The whole world is crazy."

And Mom pressed her lips tight and nodded in agreement. *"Okay, pero hay locos y hay locos,"* she said, excusing herself as not being as crazy as Taína's mother or the rest of the world. "I was not crazy. I just wanted to help my friend. You know, to make it up to her for not being there for her when she wanted to sing. You know, for leaving her—for that . . . stupid musician." My mother looked at me. I was sad and she knew I was sad, and she was sad, too.

"But it's more than that." Mom said that really fast, as if she needed to get it all out of herself before she changed her mind. "I didn't want you going down there because Inelda did it. *Ella lo hizo*. Right after she had Taína she did it. And I went with her. I didn't talk her out of it. I went with her. I knew where to go because *tú sabe'*." Mom's eyes were on the floor. "We were both raised—" She swallowed and picked up in midsentence: "Puerto Rico was full of women, so many that *la operación* begins to feel like it's nothing." At that moment that word hung in the room like a mist that refuses to die when the humidity is as thick as a wall. "It did not affect me the way it affected Inelda. When Inelda began talking to herself, I took her to see Peta Ponce. She had helped me after you were born, after I did it." She stood still, sitting on my bed. Mom was breathing deeply, but she was not yet crying, though I knew it was coming. "I didn't tell the elders," she said, and I knew why: she would have been kicked out of the church. Looking at the floor where I had thrown my dirty socks, she didn't say anything for a few endless seconds and just sat there. "Your father knows, of course." She finally found my eyes. "I was worried that with more children and him not holding jobs, you know, I was scared. After you I was scared." And I knew that after that she had shut down. There was no need or use for me to press her on anything.

"Ma," I said, "it's okay." And I embraced my mother. Her eyes were wet and she could not speak, but that was okay. There was nothing more she needed to tell me or anyone else.

"Ma," I whispered, "Peta Ponce is downstairs."

Verse 4

TAÍNA WAS IN my house. My father was so nice to her. Every second he kept asking her if she was comfortable. If she needed water. If she needed something to eat. And it made me happy to see my father fall for Taína, too, in his own way. My father had cooked all these great dishes from both Puerto Rico and Ecuador. They sat at our dinner table waiting for Peta Ponce, Doña Flores, and my mother to come out of the bathroom, because that was where Peta Ponce said the spirits wanted the women to talk things over.

I was sitting next to Taína in the living room. The last dog, which I could not find the reward flyer for to save my life, was barking happily.

The women in the bathroom were loudly whispering.

We could hear them murmuring at the past.

My father, Taína, and I tried to pay no mind to what was happening in the bathroom. In his broken English, Pops asked Taína if she felt okay. If she wanted to eat.

"Sí, muchas gracias," she said, very un-Taína-like.

My father went to make Taína a plate, but only for her;

the rest of us would have to wait till the *misa* was over. And Taína held my hand.

"I liked your stupid story. Stupid but kinda pretty," Taína said.

"What story?" my father asked, and then thought again. "Oh, the revolution in the body, yes, yes. *Claro.*" He coughed, because he never believed. He was free to understand it any way he wanted.

"I always knew you were looking at me." Her face got really close to mine and she whispered in my ear, "But I let you." And my world became new.

Doña Flores and my mother were both yelling about their youth, things and events we could barely make out. There was pounding on the walls and yells and screams in English, Spanish, and Spanglish as I heard, *"Yo te trasteo."* My mom yelled that she trusted Peta Ponce and her friend.

The loud voices coming from the closed bathroom door were too much for my father. He breathed out an uncomfortable sigh because this had all been my mother's idea.

"Pa," I said, "it's not as crazy as it sounds."

"You think so?" he said in Spanish, smirking.

"Okay, well, this is how Mom deals with her mental stuff, this is her shrink."

"Where are these spirits?" My father's mocking tone was becoming more and more impatient. He had not seen any ghosts, only a black, dwarfed woman with a hunchback, who had locked his wife and her friend in the bathroom. And worse, the dishes he had cooked were getting cold.

"They are all around us." Taína's voice was laced with sarcasm. "They are making faces at you right this minute and you don't even know it." She laughed, but my father didn't think it was funny.

"Bah." My father had seen enough. He went to where the little dog was and put the leash on. "I'll be back when this is over."

I was now alone with Taína. Her stomach was almost ready to set Usmaíl free. I wanted to kiss her. She knew I wanted to kiss her, but it was nice just to be sitting in my living room with her.

"You knew I was looking at you?"

"Of course, shithead, and you give the worst foot rubs. My feet were hurting more afterward than before your dumb-ass massage. Fuck, you are the worst," she said.

The yelling stopped. We heard a faucet turn on and the extension of a shower curtain. We heard Peta Ponce say words we could not make out.

When it was all over, three women came out of that bathroom, wet and new. All walked into Mom's room to change and eat.

In Spanish, as that was all she spoke, Peta Ponce told my mother and Doña Flores that their wounds were deep and that seeking a mental health expert would be a good thing. Peta Ponce said not to be misled by how generous the spirits were today, that things could fall apart at any given time. And so to continue seeking help. My mother looked my way because it was now her turn to see a shrink.

"I'll go with you, Ma," I said, and she just made a face.

And then Peta Ponce began to laugh. A low, continual laugh. None of us knew what to make of it. So we laughed, too. We were all laughing, with a bunch of untouched food in front of us, waiting for my father so we could all eat. Peta Ponce laughed. And the phone rang. We were one of the last families in Spanish Harlem to actually have a landline. Peta Ponce pointed at the phone.

My mother picked the phone up.

My father had been arrested.

Verse 5

MY FATHER HAD wandered down to the Upper East Side. Someone had recognized the dog. I had to confess so he could be set free. I was taken into a room for questioning. Cops put handcuffs on me even though there was nowhere to go. I was surrounded by like twenty cops standing around a kid. They were congratulating themselves. They took pictures with me. This was the guy we were after. This was the guy stealing all those dogs. We got him. And none of those cops went off to fight real crime. They just stuck around as if I were a powerful superhero with a cape and needed heavy security. The people whose dogs I had been borrowing were mostly powerful Upper East Side women. They were powerful because they were married to powerful Upper East Side men. These women didn't really work. They just attended these New York society parties. They also made sure all of New York City knew about my crime. Lots of camera crews, *The New York Times* had sent reporters to cover the story. The *New York Post* brought my father into it with the headline SON OF BITCH. Reporters and photographers were everywhere.

Then a white, heavy detective walked in. He had a potbelly and smelled of sweat. Then he placed a knife on the table.

"Is this your knife?" Though he must have known it was because he must have searched my room.

"Yes," I said, "that is my knife."

"Why do you carry a knife?"

"To cut the leashes," I said.

"But leashes are made of metal. You need a wire cutter. So why do you carry a knife? To kill people?"

"Not leashes bought by rich women, those are expensive, made of fine leather. They can easily be cut with a simple kitchen knife." Which was what he had there.

He made a fake sound like this made no sense. "How many dogs you stole?"

"Zero," I said politely. "I brought them all back."

"You're a punk kid." He gave up. "You'll get what's coming to you." And he left the room. The other twenty cops never asked me anything. They continued to stand there as if waiting for backup.

Soon I had to be transferred. Escorted by the lobby of the station house, I saw the potbellied detective again. He was not after me but out to please all these wealthy women. He assured them that I would get jail time. That it was up to them to press charges. They in turn told him they would let their husbands know what a great, great job he had done in capturing that Dogman who had brought so much havoc and destruction to their lives.

The cops took me outside. A mob awaited me. I tried to find my parents, Sal, or Taína in the crowd, with no luck. Lots of yelling, cruelty this, cruelty that. I waited for a paddy wagon to come and take me to the Tombs. One reporter, whom I recognized because I had seen him on television, got close enough to ask me a question.

"How do you feel about your mother?"

"I feel very proud of her."

"Then why'd you do it?"

"To help. To help people I care about."

And the reporter looked at me as if this were not what I was supposed to say.

The paddy wagon arrived, and they put me inside it. It drove away, sirens screaming like there was a fire ahead.

At the Tombs' entrance there was another mob.

"You miserable piece of shit!" Some half-naked woman holding a PETA sign threw a pork chop at my face. I thought it was a waste of food.

Inside, I was placed in a big room, sort of like a little courtroom, and told to wait there with ten other cops who had nothing better to do than guard a handcuffed teen. The wealthy women whose dogs I had borrowed waited outside the big room. Some were even smoking, disregarding the sign, and the cops let them. These wealthy women were angry. They said I had brutally violated them without their consent. I had misinformed them. I had coerced them. Had fooled them. I had not given them the proper information. I had left these wealthy women emotionally scarred for life. They would never be the same again. I had humiliated them, brought shame, and their wounds were so deep they could never continue to live their lives in the same way again.

The women entered. I expected to see my parents. But the cops wouldn't let them in. The room was large with benches where the rich women sat. I was seated, still handcuffed, when Ms. Cahill walked in and sat next to me. I was very happy to see her. Like all of New York City, she had already heard about the Dogman. She had taken a day off teaching to come to my defense. Ms. Cahill told me not to be afraid. That she was going to speak on my behalf. If these women didn't press charges, I would be free to go. She said to let her do the talking; it was a matter of making these women see the flip side of the coin. Ms. Cahill had done this for other students, I was sure, because the potbellied detective wanted to speak to the women first.

"Don't let the real issues here sway you," he said. "Stick to the facts. Don't consider things that evoke sympathy or emotions. Leave leniency and compassion to the jury. If you press charges, society will put this man—and make no mistake, he is a man, not a kid, a man—on trial."

The women nodded and the potbellied detective gave way for Ms. Cahill to speak, referring to her as Megan, so he must have known her.

"The facts are that you lost something you can always get back and you have enough of, which is your wealth," she said. "All your dogs were unharmed and returned."

But the women were still angry. It was when Ms. Cahill began to speak with a touch of a poet that the women's expressions changed. "This is a brilliant kid, far more unique than any of us in this room." Some women bobbed their heads. "Julio Colmiñares never began at the starting line, like you and I did. He began back there. And yet"—Ms. Cahill dug into her purse and brought out my report card—"he has the grades to get him into college." She passed my report card around. Some women looked at it and nodded before passing it forward. "In Julio Colmiñares saving himself—he saves all of us." She walked over to where the women were sitting. "If we intend for our society, our city, to grow, then we begin here, with this boy. You, sweet ladies, are intelligent women, fashioned by a humanist culture that strongly believes that in aesthetics there is meaning. So that in the Met, in the MoMA, in Lincoln Center, in all these things you ladies love, there is not just beauty but transcendence. But what does it mean, finding transcendence in beautiful things, if you cannot find it in yourselves to forgive?" She paused. "And so, sweet ladies, I give this boy to you, and I beg you to give this boy back to us."

All the women pressed charges.

My rights were read.

I was booked.

Mom emptied out her boot.

She paid my bail.

I went home and waited for my trial.

THE LAST BOOK OF JULIO

USMAÍL

SIEMPRE QUE SE HACE UNA HISTORIA SE HABLA DE UN VIEJO DE UN NIÑO O DE SÍ.

—SILVIO RODRÍGUEZ

Coda

THAT NIGHT I couldn't sleep. While my parents slept like rocks, something told me to get out of bed and look out the window. From the tenth floor down, I saw a demon. A devil standing by the mailbox. The devil was waving at me frantically to come down. To leave my bed and join him that night. Salvador was in full, multicolored costume, with horned mask, jumpsuit, cape, and everything. I was so happy to see el Vejigante.

I snuck out. Took the elevator down and joined him by the mailbox.

"Where you been?" I said.

"Visiting graves," he said from behind his mask. I guessed he had had a change of heart and had gone to apologize to those he had hurt, even if it would not bring them back or change the past.

"It's Labor Day, *papo,*" he said, removing his mask.

"It's May," I said.

"No, not that. Taína."

My heart began pounding.

"What, what hospital? Where?" I was ready to follow el Vejigante anywhere.

"What hospital, Sal?" Even if my parents would kill me, I was ready to miss school and stay with her until Usmaíl was born.

"Peta Ponce is with her. She said doctors treat pregnant women like they have a disease and not like it's the most natural thing in the world."

"She's giving birth at home?" I was about to cross the street. Head to Taína's house, where I expected Peta Ponce to be by her side. Salvador saw how anxious I was.

"Relax, *papo*. Relax and follow me."

The casita was a shanty built on a vacant lot on 111th Street and Madison Avenue. Once, there stood a Buster Brown shoe store. Where many newly arrived Puerto Ricans and other immigrants from the 1940s all the way to the 1990s would buy shoes on layaway. Next to that store there had once been a botanica. Next to that a mom-and-pop restaurant with a sign in Spanish: IF YOUR WIFE CAN'T COOK, DON'T GET A DIVORCE. COME EAT HERE. All that was left from those bygone times when immigrants came dreaming of their sons hired by the men their fathers worked for, dreaming of their daughters sleeping in the houses their mothers cleaned, all of what was left of that time was the casita. The vacant lot had been cleared and fenced. The shanty had been steadily and firmly erected on that site. It had been painted in bright colors. It boasted four windows and a veranda halfway across the front entrance. A sign hung from the door: *UN PEDACITO DE PUERTO RICO*. The casita was made entirely of wood, with a large tin-sheet roof. The windows didn't completely fit the frames, but they served their purpose by opening and closing to let both air and sunlight in. Outside there was a neat garden with rows of sprouting vegetables and herbs. There were roosters and chickens running along with dogs and cats that chewed the basil and mint. Outside the fence, on the sidewalk, was a broken lamppost where a raccoon was sleeping, curled inside where years of rust had created a big hole inside the metal post.

The old man who had built the casita was wearing a white *guayabera* and a *jíbaro* hat. He was poor and never harmed anyone in his life. Santos Malànguez was his name, and he had known Peta Ponce since he was a boy back on the island.

The casita had no plumbing, but it was clean. There was a pullout sofa, a small dresser, and a bathtub by the corner. The walls were decorated with posters of different towns in Puerto Rico: Cabo Rojo, Fajardo, Bayamón, Mayagüez, Carolina, Loíza Aldea, Ponce, Aguadilla, Santurce, Guayama, the island of Vieques and its little sister of Culebra, and, of course, San Juan, the capital. There was a dirty map of the New York City subway system, where someone had scribbled, *"El barrio más grande de Puerto Rico, Nueva Yol."*

Taína was inside, standing and breathing in and out. Peta Ponce instructed her to walk around inside the tiny casita.

"We should be at a hospital," I said to Peta Ponce.

"No," Peta Ponce said firmly in Spanish, *"aquí, aquí está perfecto."*

"Fuck! Fuck, this shit sucks." Taína kept cursing in between breaths and gritted teeth. Peta Ponce asked her if she wanted to go back outside for some fresh air. "Fuck, yeah," she moaned as the pains were getting worse.

"Where's Doña Flores?" I asked Peta Ponce. Peta Ponce said that just like when this began Inelda was asleep, so she needed to be asleep when it ended.

The weather was beautiful. New York City was quiet, like it was waiting for something wonderful.

"Peta," Taína said, breathing in deeply, "I think I need to lay the fuck back down." I helped Peta Ponce bring Taína back inside the casita.

Salvador helped me pull the sofa out into a bed. Once unfolded, it ate up most of the space inside the casita. Peta Ponce looked in the drawers and found clean sheets and a pillow and she made the bed. I helped Peta Ponce lay Taína on the sofa bed. Taína's eyes were bulging and her moaning became louder and longer. Peta Ponce looked at a man's watch she had on her wrist. *"Mija, tus dolores están llegando ma' y ma' cerca,"* she said, and gave Taína water. With the sofa bed now opened and the bathtub by the corner, the casita was crowded.

"'fuera! 'fuera!" Peta Ponce ordered Salvador and me to go outside.

"'Pera, Salvador," Peta Ponce said to el Vejigante, *"vete a buscar a Willie."*

Sal left to go find this person.

Taína was sweating.

"Y tú . . ." She ordered me to go to the bodega, buy a bottle of Coke, a gallon of milk, empty both, and bring them to her.

I rushed out to do as told.

I opened the fence, crossed the street, and went inside a twenty-four-hour bodega. When I returned, after having emptied both contents, Peta Ponce took only the empty Coke.

"Mira, así, ¿ve'?" Placing the hollow bottle to her mouth, Peta Ponce blew on it like it was a flute. *"Así. Ve', así, mija."* She handed the bottle to Taína, who began to blow inside the mouth of the bottle. The bottle began to whistle. The whistling was comforting, and it seemed never to rise but instead stay at a steady pace. Taína blew on the bottle, and it seemed to calm her down some.

I went back out to give Peta Ponce enough room.

"Mira, mijo," Peta Ponce said through an open window. She told me to fill up the steel drum that lay by the fence with water and start a fire underneath it. I didn't have a wrench to open the fire hydrant on the sidewalk or a lighter or anything.

Peta Ponce knew this because she went into her black purse and emptied it all out on the casita's dirt floor. There was a cross, a picture of a saint, a toothbrush, a cigar, tissues, condoms, a cell phone, herbs, mints, and a cigar. She rummaged through the stuff till she found a lighter and a wrench. Through the open window she gave it to me.

With the wrench I opened a fire hydrant across the street. I filled and emptied the gallon of milk several times until the steel drum was full. The drum stood on top of two deftly spread-out cinder blocks in order to make a perfect nest underneath it for firewood. I gathered fallen branches on the ground and started a fire. I heated the water, and when the temperature was just right, Peta Ponce told me to transfer the hot water to the tub inside. Once again, I continually filled and emptied the milk gallon, making several trips inside the casita to empty the hot water into the tub. After a few trips, the tub was filled with hot water. Peta Ponce took away the bottle that a sweaty Taína had been blowing into. I joined Peta Ponce back inside the casita. I helped her in getting Taína up from the sofa bed. Peta Ponce helped Taína disrobe. Seeing Taína naked for the first time did nothing. All I wanted was for Taína to no longer be in pain.

Peta Ponce and I gently lifted and sat Taína's naked body in the tub. "*Coño,* it's fucking hot!" Taína yelled, tears flowing.

"Mejor, mija," Peta Ponce said, sounding like our parents.

"Too fucking hot, Julio," Taína pleaded, as if I could override Peta Ponce's method. "It's too hot. Son of a bitch, shit, it's hot!" she cried. Though it hurt me, I stayed silent. I trusted Peta Ponce like my mother had trusted her and like all those other women had trusted Peta Ponce.

"It's okay, Taína," I said, "Peta Ponce knows what she's doing."

Taína couldn't have cared less and continued to curse in pain. She sat in the bathtub in an upright position. Peta Ponce made her drink more water. Peta Ponce told her to open her legs more, *más, más, más.* Taína kept yelling the water was hot. Peta Ponce said, Open your legs, *mija,* more, more, so the heat of the water can penetrate your insides, relax your body, *mija*. Let the hot water open the door for Usmaíl to walk through.

The pains became stronger.

The contractions were more frequent, and Taína yelled.

"I'm gonna fucking die. Fuck, I'm gonna fucking die!"

"Nadie se muere, mi bella." Peta Ponce reassured Taína that many claim to be midwives, but all they do is make angels. I do not deliver angels, she said. Taína kept cursing.

"¡Puñeta, me muero!" yelled Taína.

"Mea, mea . . ." Peta Ponce kept repeating to Taína to try to pee. "Can you pee? Pee, *mija,* pee in the water. It would be good if you could pee," Peta Ponce said.

Taína moaned in between tears and breaths. It took a while, but Taína peed. Along with her urine were little strings of blood running out of her like entrails. Peta Ponce said this was a good thing. Her cervix was opening. Usmaíl was on the other side. Peta Ponce told me to find a twelve-inch stick from the many fallen branches out in the garden. When I gave it to her, she dipped it in water to clean it a bit and placed it in Taína's mouth. She bit it hard, and it helped to calm her.

I then helped Peta Ponce carry Taína out of the tub. She dried Taína up and I helped to gently lay Taína back on the sofa bed. I emptied the tub, once again coming in and out of the casita, filling and emptying the plastic milk gallon. Once done I joined Peta Ponce and Taína back inside the casita. I heard the fence gate slam.

Salvador and a man with a fuzzy beard and droopy eyes walked in through the gate and into the garden. "Peta Ponce,

I'm here." From outside by the garden. "It is me, Willie. You need me, Peta?" With respect he bowed to the old woman.

"No sé," Peta Ponce said. *"Quizá."* She told Willie to stand by, that this birth was stuck in time.

"I got wha'ever you need, Doña Ponce," Willie said. "I got it. I got needles, big ones, too. I got the street equal to Stadol. I got serious painkillers, too, or anything else you need to numb her. I got it." Peta Ponce answered to this dealer that every labor had a beginning and an end but that Taína's was stuck in the middle. And to just stand by.

"I'll be outside," Willie said calmly, and this told me that Peta Ponce and that guy had done this many times. Sal, too, waited silently next to Willie outside.

"Suave, suave, mija. Mira . . ." Peta Ponce softly brushed Taína's hair and told her that if the pain got to be too much, she might have to give her some drugs. Inject her, she told her. The big needle is going to hurt, but then Taína will feel nothing. But that they should wait, just a bit more.

Still biting the stick, Taína said, "Don't fucking wait! I don't give a fuck. Give me the drugs." Taína wanted the pains to go away. "Give it to me. Just give me the fucking shot. Give me the drugs."

But Peta Ponce did no such thing. That was only a last resort. She understood Taína's pain, but it would be over soon. She ordered me to wait outside. And then in a soothing voice that resembled nothing coming out of her misshapen body, Peta Ponce whispered to Taína that this casita she built with Santos Malànguez many years ago, this casita was the last link to a time when old people like her were young. They arrived in a new country, in these new cities, on cold days. But in the summer they joined together in casitas. We built them on vacant lots to celebrate and dance, she said. The birth of your child is a celebration. And she kissed Taína's sweaty face. "*Este bohío es donde Usmaíl tiene que nacer, mija,*" she said.

And then she spat the stick away, and during one of Taína's loudest curses, a tiny skull covered in black fuzz appeared from Taína's cervix.

"*Ven,*" Peta Ponce ordered Usmaíl. "*Ven, sale, que el mundo es bello.*" But it did not move any farther.

Me, Salvador, and Willie were looking in through the windows from outside the casita. Peta Ponce called for only me to come inside. I helped Peta Ponce get Taína out of the bed. We held her up. Peta Ponce told Taína to squat. To stand with both legs apart. To let gravity help you, *mija.* I held on to Taína from the right side and Peta Ponce held her from the left so she wouldn't tip over while squatting.

Taína squatted and Peta Ponce told me to stand behind Taína and hold her tightly. I held a squatting Taína from behind, my arms around her pregnant waist. Peta Ponce then let go of Taína and lay on the floor, on her back, looking up at Taína's cervix. From the floor and looking up to Taína's womb, Peta Ponce reached out with both hands, placing one on each side between Taína's legs, and Peta Ponce widened the passage. "*Asi, puja, mija,*" Peta Ponce said, and Taína pushed, and then with infinite delicacy, Peta Ponce took hold of the fragile, tiny crown and with very accurate skill and confidence brought Usmaíl's little head out into the light of day.

"*Así, así, así, muy bien, muy bien,*" Peta Ponce said, still on her back, on the floor, looking up at Taína's womb. She held the baby's head and eased out the rest of Usmaíl's body coated in Taína's blood. Peta Ponce's teeth bit the cord free and with one last push and a loud curse, Taína expelled the placenta.

Outside.

Willie heard the baby. He quickly took out his pocketknife and lighter. He placed the blade to the flame and then passed the hot knife to Peta Ponce through the opened window. Peta sanitized the cord she had bit free and tied it up with the knife's tip. With a damp cloth she cleaned Usmaíl just a bit and handed the baby to Taína.

"Bien hecho, mija. 'Tá ma' bella, tu nena," she said to Taína, who took her daughter in her arms and smiled, laughed, and cried and laughed again.

Outside the dogs barked, the cats meowed, the raccoons looked through garbage, the red-tailed hawks flew, the rats and roaches rummaged, the whores hustled, the thieves stole, the drug dealers peddled, the cops walked their beats, the yuppies danced, ate, and drank, immigrants worked, and worked, and worked, fathers worked, mothers worked, kids went to school—all of Spanish Harlem wasn't any different from any other night.

From outside by the garden, both Willie the dealer and Salvador Negron, the Capeman, bowed to me, and I returned their gesture as they made their way home and away from the light. Sal paused for just a second, as if he were going to tell me something, but picked up his pace again.

Peta Ponce wiped the sweat off her brow and whispered

to herself or to the spirits that just as when we are born there are people waiting for us, there will be people waiting for us when we die. And for the first time that night, her eyes found mine and she said that it is easier to build good children than to fix broken adults.

And I understood her. Usmaíl was the greatest gift the inner universe could have given Taína and all of us. I will never forget the first time Usmaíl saw the light of day, how she cried so loudly, as if letting the inner heavens know that she had arrived. As if she wanted all the atoms in the universe to hear that the revolution was a success. It was a revolution. One that would not betray itself. Usmaíl cried and cried, and Taína drank more water, ate half a sandwich, breastfed Usmaíl, and later both mother and daughter stretched, yawned, and, exhausted, crashed into a deep inner sleep.

THE THREE WOMEN became a welcomed and sought-after sight in Spanish Harlem. Taína and her mother easily spoke to each other and to anyone who wanted to see Usmaíl. Who wanted to see the baby. You could easily find the women on the street, mother clutching daughter, daughter pushing stroller, making the necessary visits to the supermarket and the Check-O-Mate for welfare benefits or a movie theater, a bakery, or a beauty salon. The women were living among a sea of regular people doing their best to get by, and it seemed that even among crowds nothing could ever disturb their smiles. Not catcalls from the corner boys directed at Taína: *"Mira, ¿to' eso tuyo?"* Fuck you, Taína would shoot back, and keep pushing her stroller. Nor gossip from laundromat women directed at Doña Flores.

When Taína did return to school, she sat alongside other teen mothers discussing baby bargains or baby clothes or just talking high school teenage stuff. Taína never cared for clothes, makeup, popularity, or anything. Like her mother, she would smile when smiled at, as if her smile were telling you she was not your enemy and it was up to you to be her friend, if you were nice. The boys liked her, they all fell in love, and I was no different. And like everyone else, I was waiting to hear Taína sing.

IT WAS THE summer night when the most powerful of meteor showers that have ever been recorded in New York City occurred. Not even the lights could darken those shooting stars. Their quick glows were long and lasting, as if hipster angels were being cast out of heaven and hurled down to earth. A tidal wave of heat had engulfed the city, too, and everyone just wanted relief and took to the streets.

On that same night, Carlito's Café and Galeria on 107th Street and Lexington Avenue, which was owned by a kind Andean woman from La Paz, Bolivia, named Eliana Godoy, was the coolest place to be. She had named the café after her father and on the walls were paintings by local artists, but what everyone always came to Carlito's for was to hear music. I'd heard Lila Downs at Carlito's, Manu Chao, Susana Baca, Tania Libertad, Gaby Moreno, Raquel Z. Rivera, Las Lolas, and Totó La Momposina, too. But that night, the night of the shooting stars, was Taína's night. Salvador installed me and my parents by a small table in the corner. My mother was happy, my father held her hand. The café was half-full. I spotted Taína reading some sheet music, in a tight red dress, all legs and curves, looking like nobody's mother. She spotted me, kissed her hand, blew me a kiss, and went back to her thing. The musicians at the small stage were standing around one another, clowning, laughing, their drinks on the floor next to them. Usmaíl was out, in another world; she dreamed in her stroller next to Doña Flores sitting by a table across from us.

Soon.

All kinds of shuffles, coughs, the bartender getting in last drinks, followed by a slow silence.

Salvador strode up to the piano and sat down in front of the keys. There was a quiet stir before he firmly but gently ran his fingers over them. Taína stood alone in front of an old microphone. A humid light from the window framed Taína's lovely face. When her first low and sad note was born, a great silence overtook the café like the first drop before the heavens opened. Taína began to sing sad words whose weeping was buried inside a melody. A song that we had been hearing all our lives, had grown up with, but it was only through her voice that we began to understand it. Taína's song revealed that we suffer because we do not submit to one another's love. When kissed, we pretend to be moved, but it's really more a sense of duty. Taína sang that like children, like books, love has become the dust of the world. And when her voice sweetly hummed that all the kisses we did not give will one day be given, that's when I knew that everyone in Carlito's Café was seeing whom they loved. It was the dead everyone loved. It was the dead everyone missed. In the people's eyes were images of faces that had once held their hands, taken their vows, changed their diapers, their clothes, or simply saw their first smiles and footsteps but were no longer living. Love is not a prisoner of time, Taína's voice sang, love does not recognize death, it is not under its authority. Her voice sang that the unstoppable river that flows among us is not time but love. Taína was throwing it all to the fire so that it could be wholly consumed and, therefore, live forever. She was calm, composed, and older, and when her voice deepened, tightened, sailed higher, filling the air with an intense sense of triumph—everyone began to cry. Her voice contained all our suffering, all our failures, and all our joys. I saw Salvador Negron, el Vejigante, the Capeman, leader of the Vampires, the man who like shattered pieces of glass in a kaleidoscope had reappeared with new faces, but always sad, guilt-ridden, and suffering, was now transfigured into that of a sixteen-year-old kid. He struck the piano keys with a subtle bliss, as if the dead were whispering in his ear that it was okay, they understood.

Doña Flores's chest was a peacock. This was her voice, too. It was Taína offering all the kisses Doña Flores never had a chance to give. Her daughter filled her singing lungs with air like that night years ago at Orchestra Records. This was the bridge that Inelda Flores had started to build, and now her daughter, Taína, was completing it so that we could all walk across it.

In Taína's voice I did see whom I loved and who loved me back, but it was not Taína. Whom I saw was my mother. I saw her dreams, I saw my father's dreams, too. They were trampled and unfinished. Their feet and hands were calloused from the stones they had pushed and the cement sidewalks they had walked upon barefoot. Taína's voice told me that my parents had not given up, that they had passed these dreams down. I was to push the rock farther and my children's children were to do the same.

And when Taína threw her head back, breathed deeply, closed her eyes, and held on to a single note that seemed it would not end until the Second Coming, everyone gasped for air like when something is so astonishing, so miraculous, it cannot be true. Then slowly her voice rocked itself back and forth, back and forth, back to earth. If a swan could be more than what it already is, Taína had been that.

Then, gradually, the piano went silent. Salvador was spent and drank some water. He hobbled back to a chair, reeling, and rocking, he unsteadily sat down and grabbed his chest. But the old man was smiling as if he knew he was going to die tonight, he was going out with music. Taína drank water, checked on Usmaíl in her stroller. All her rebellious atoms in her infant body were calm and asleep. Dreaming and plotting endless possibilities inside a body with no king or god. The revolution was alive, but right now it had traveled, so it rested. Next to the stroller was Usmaíl's grandmother, happy and alive, singing again through her daughter.

Soon three congas slowly drummed themselves into the

piano's vacuum. The *congeros'* hands started to bang away. Taína kissed her sleeping daughter good night and joined them back onstage. Taína began dancing to *jíbaro,* Afro-Cuban, *plena, bomba,* and *santero*-rooted music. Her hands moved outward and forward in sync with her hips, eyes looking up to the heavens. The rhythm of the congas raced to match the sways, and the people cleared their eyes and began to shake. The people began to clap. The people began to stomp. The people began to quicken their thighs. When two trumpets, one sax, a trombone, bass, *timbalero,* and two *cuatros* joined in, it was Taína's cue for her voice to transform into a *le-lo-lai*. The blood pressure rose, the heat sailed.

Carlito's Café shuddered like an entire planet trembling. From outside, some yuppies must have heard Taína's singing, as the café was soon overflowing with yoga mats galore. The yuppies were quaking, rubbing against one another's sweaty hipster clothes.

And the walls of Carlito's Café were about to crash down, as the place was jammed so tight that the doors and windows had to be opened. The cold, air-conditioned air had no business being there that night, and it quickly evaporated into the humid summer that flowed and swirled around hot bodies. A thick wind of kindness spun itself around the people. Some shook so fast that they would not stop until something within them told them to pass out. They fell as others picked them up and gave them water.

Taína's voice climbed and then seeped down, burying itself inside our cells. Soon, five women dressed in all white with tambourines joined Taína's side. They sang, but Taína quickly drowned their voices and they knew their rightful place was as a backup chorus of *santeras*. And then the melody effortlessly picked up speed, as if Taína's voice held the band's hand and told them to run with her. Told the people to follow her. Her voice was telling us we were all free and that she needed us to run with her so she could be free, too.

Taína had the band reacting to her improvisations, and then, with eyes closed and body swaying like the Brooklyn Bridge, Taína took the band to a place only she knew. And everyone followed.

I looked out the window.

I saw Peta Ponce. Her feet moved up and down like those of a marionette, as if she had strings tied to her joints and some invisible hand was controlling her from above. The *espiritista*'s dance held this unbearable awkward grace as Spanish Harlem was drenched with people of every color, gender, sexual orientation, and income bracket. The spine, the backbone of the world, its *cordillera,* the Latin American continent, was represented in the streets, holding up the bones of every Latina group, offering a healthy skeleton of possibilities. The conquerors were there, too, as I saw Spaniards holding up their flag while they opened wine bottles, cheese, and bread they shared with everyone.

Children took to the sidewalks with chalks and paint. Men danced with men, women danced with one another, and sometimes they switched. A squad car appeared. A young cop stepped out with Ms. Cahill, they swayed, they shook, they shuddered, they shimmied, and the fire hydrants on that block gave out. With smiles on their faces, the people stretched out their arms and took in the drizzle. The sky continued to rain fire as the meteor shower intensified like it wanted to ignite the moon into a new sun. Every tenement fire escape was teeming with white drying laundry and bodies who felt they had wings and could fly above the projects.

That night when Taína sang, no one had credit card debt, no one had rents to pay, no one had ills or imperfections, no one knew the meaning of sad words, no one remembered winter. Everyone got paid, the right way. Everyone was young. Everyone built a ladder to the stars. Everyone did for others what they wanted done for themselves. Everyone was in love. Everyone saw who loved them. Everyone had been forgiven.